ECHOES OF RESILIENCE

Echoes of Resilience

My Journey of Trials and Redemption

Eric J. Medina

CONTENTS

Reflection of
the Rain

The rain fell in sheets, drenching the pavement and reflecting the challenges within. Each drop seemed to embody the relentless trials that had shaped my path. Standing on the edge of a crowded street, I couldn't help but reflect on how far I had come. The journey had been anything but easy—filled with shattered dreams, fractured relationships, and moments when hope seemed like a distant memory.

But amid the storm, there was a whisper of resilience that refused to be silenced. It was in the quiet moments of solitude, amidst the chaos of life's challenges, that I found the strength to endure. This was not just a story of survival; it was a testament to the human spirit's capacity to rise, even when everything seemed to conspire against it.

The city bustled around me, a constant reminder of life's unpredictable nature. People hurried past, lost in their worlds of ambition and struggle. I watched them, wondering if they too carried their echoes of resilience, hidden beneath the facade of daily life.

Yet, despite the throngs of people, a profound sense of loneliness often enveloped me. It was an invisible shroud, heavy and suffocating, that lingered even amid a crowd. Loneliness wasn't just the absence of company; it was the absence of connection, the aching void where understanding and empathy should have been. I felt like an island in an endless sea, isolated and adrift.

There were nights when the silence was deafening, when the weight of my thoughts pressed down with an unbearable intensity. The four walls of my room seemed to close in, amplifying the solitude that clung to me like a shadow. Friends and loved ones were physically present, but the emotional distance felt insurmountable. It was as if I were speaking a different language, one that only I could understand.

I recalled a moment from years ago, a turning point when I faced a devastating loss that shook me to the core. It was then that I realized the depth of my resilience, forged in the crucible of grief and uncertainty. The echoes of that experience reverberated through my life, shaping my decisions and guiding me toward a path of healing and renewal.

As I took a deep breath and stepped forward, the rain continued to fall, cleansing the streets and washing away the remnants of doubt and fear. Each step was a testament to my journey, a journey marked by resilience, courage, and the unwavering belief that even in the darkest of times, there is always a glimmer of hope. The journey ahead was uncertain and filled with new challenges and opportunities for growth.

Yet, I carried with me the echoes of resilience—a reminder of my inner strength and the power to overcome. With each chapter yet unwritten, I embraced the promise of tomorrow, knowing that every trial would only add to the tapestry of my resilience.

Despite the loneliness, I found solace in small, unexpected places. A smile from a stranger, a kind word from a colleague, or a moment of clarity during a quiet walk in the park. These brief instances of connection reminded me that I was not entirely alone and that my story was interwoven with the stories of others, each of us struggling and striving in our ways.

I began to seek out these moments, to create connections where once there had been none. Volunteering at a local shelter, joining a book club, and opening up to new friendships. Slowly, the walls of loneliness began to crumble, replaced by a sense of community and belonging.

Every interaction, every shared experience, became a thread in the fabric of my resilience. I learned that true connection required vulnerability, the courage to share my struggles, and to listen to the struggles of others. In doing so, I discovered a profound truth: that in our shared humanity, we find the strength to overcome even the deepest loneliness.

One evening, as I sat in my small apartment, I received an unexpected call. It was from an old friend I hadn't spoken to in years. We had drifted apart, life taking us in different directions, but hearing her voice brought a flood of memories and emotions. We talked for hours, sharing our journeys, our struggles, and our triumphs. It was as if no time had passed, and the connection we had once cherished was still there, stronger than ever.

This reconnection was a turning point. It made me realize that while loneliness can feel like an insurmountable wall, the smallest act of reaching out can begin to dismantle it. The conversation with my friend reignited a spark within me, a reminder that connections, both old and new, were within reach if I dared to seek them out.

Inspired by this, I made a conscious effort to reconnect with other friends and family members. I reached out to those I had lost touch with, apologizing for my absence and sharing my desire to rebuild our relationships. The responses were overwhelmingly positive. People were more understanding and forgiving than I had imagined.

They, too, had faced their battles with loneliness and were eager to rekindle the bonds we once shared. As these connections flourished, I found myself surrounded by a supportive network. We shared our joys and sorrows, lifting each other during difficult times and celebrating our victories, no matter how small. This newfound sense of community was a balm for my loneliness, healing wounds I had long thought permanent.

Through this journey, I discovered that resilience is not a solitary endeavor. It is strengthened by the connections we make, and the love and support we give and receive. In embracing vulnerability and reaching out to others, I found a profound sense of belonging and the courage to face whatever challenges lay ahead.

With each new day, I continued to build on these connections, finding strength in the shared experiences and the unwavering support of those around me. The echoes of resilience, once a solitary whisper, had become a powerful chorus, guiding me toward a future filled with hope, love, and endless possibilities.

SHATTERED ILLUSIONS

The sun rose hesitantly over the city, its pale light filtering through the gray clouds that still lingered from the previous night's storm. The streets, now drying, bore the faint reflections of puddles, remnants of the rain that had washed away the dust and grime. As I walked through the familiar pathways of my daily routine, I felt a sense of renewal, as if the city and I were both emerging from a long, shared struggle.

Despite the newfound connections and the budding sense of community, there were moments when the past resurfaced, bringing with it the pain and disillusionment of broken dreams. It was in these moments that I confronted the deeper, unresolved facets of my journey, the parts that required more than just resilience—they demanded a confrontation with the illusions I had once held dear.

One of the most significant illusions was the belief that love could conquer all. I had entered relationships with the naive hope that love would be enough to overcome any obstacle. But reality had a different lesson in store. Love, while powerful, was not always sufficient to bridge the gaps created by fundamental differences, unhealed wounds, and personal demons.

I remembered my first serious relationship. We had been young, full of dreams and aspirations, convinced that our love was unique, invincible. For a while, it seemed to be true. We shared everything, from our deepest fears to our most cherished hopes. But as time passed, the cracks began to show. The pressures of life, career ambitions, and unspoken expectations started to erode the foundation we had built.

Arguments became more frequent, and the emotional distance grew. We tried to hold on, believing that love would see us through. But in the end, it wasn't enough. The breakup was painful, a shattering of the illusion that love alone could sustain a relationship. It was a harsh lesson, but a necessary one.

As I navigated the aftermath of that breakup, I realized that love required more than just feeling; it demanded effort, communication, and a willingness to face uncomfortable truths. It was a lesson I carried into subsequent relationships, shaping how I approached love and connection.

Another illusion that was shattered was the belief in the permanence of things. I had once thought that certain aspects of my life—career, friendships, even my sense of self—were unchangeable. But life, with its unpredictable nature, taught me otherwise. Jobs that seemed secure were lost, friendships that felt eternal faded away, and my understanding of myself evolved in ways I hadn't anticipated.

One particularly stark example was my career. I had dedicated years to climbing the corporate ladder, believing that success was measured by titles and paychecks. But as I reached the upper echelons, I found myself unfulfilled, disconnected from the passions that had once driven me. The corporate world, with its relentless demands and superficial rewards, left me feeling empty.

It was during a particularly grueling project that the realization hit me. I was working late, the office eerily quiet except for the hum of the fluorescent lights. I looked around at my colleagues, all similarly exhausted, and questioned what we were striving for.

The answer was disheartening. We were chasing an illusion of success, one that came at the cost of our well-being and happiness.

That night, I decided to reevaluate my path. I began exploring other avenues, seeking work that aligned with my values and passions. It wasn't an easy transition, and it involved financial sacrifices and moments of doubt. But it was necessary for my growth and fulfillment.

As I rebuilt my career, I found joy in unexpected places—mentoring others, engaging in creative projects, and contributing to causes I cared about. This shift not only revitalized my professional life but also brought a sense of purpose that had been missing.

These shattered illusions, though painful, were crucial in my journey of self-discovery and resilience. They stripped away the superficial layers, revealing the core of what truly mattered. Through these experiences, I learned to embrace change, to let go of the need for control, and to find strength in vulnerability.

Another profound lesson came from the illusion of control. I believed that with enough effort and planning, I could shape my life exactly as I wanted. But life, with its inherent uncertainty, showed me otherwise. The more I tried to control every detail, the more I felt the weight of frustration and disappointment when things didn't go as planned.

Learning to let go of this illusion was liberating. It allowed me to be more present, to appreciate the journey rather than fixate on the destination. I began to see challenges not as setbacks but as opportunities for growth. Each unexpected twist and turn became a part of my story, contributing to the person I was becoming.

The relationships in my life also taught me valuable lessons about expectations and acceptance. The illusion that others could fulfill all my needs or that I could meet all of theirs led to inevitable disappointment. Realizing that each person has their path and struggles, I learned to appreciate the moments of connection without imposing unrealistic expectations.

In my friendships, I started valuing quality over quantity. Deep, meaningful conversations became more important than maintaining a large social circle. I found solace in the understanding and support of a few close friends rather than spreading myself thin trying to meet the expectations of many.

Family relationships, too, were a source of both challenge and growth. The expectations placed on me, and those I placed on my family, often led to tension. But through open communication and empathy, we began to navigate these dynamics more effectively.

Understanding that we are all flawed and that perfection is an illusion helped us build stronger, more authentic connections.

As I walked through the city, now bathed in the soft morning light, I felt a sense of gratitude for the lessons learned and the resilience gained. The journey was far from over, but with each step, I moved forward with a clearer understanding of myself and the world around me.

The echoes of resilience continued to guide me, a constant reminder that even in the face of shattered illusions, there is always the possibility of renewal and growth. And with that, I welcomed the challenges and opportunities that lay ahead, ready to embrace them with an open heart and an unwavering spirit...

The Weight of Expectations

The next morning, the sunlight streamed through my window, heralding a new day. As I stretched and prepared for the day ahead, the reflections on shattered illusions lingered in my mind. They had shaped me, transformed me, and prepared me for the next phase of my journey: understanding and managing the weight of expectations.

Expectations are a double-edged sword. On one hand, they can serve as motivation, pushing us to strive for greater achievements and personal growth. On the other, they can become a source of immense pressure, leading to anxiety, self-doubt, and a constant fear of failure.

I often found myself caught in the latter. Growing up, I had internalized the expectations of those around me—parents, teachers, and society at large. The pressure to excel academically, to secure a prestigious job, and to lead a life that others deemed "successful" was overwhelming. Even as an adult, those expectations lingered, shaping my decisions and actions.

One particularly challenging aspect was the expectation of perfection. Whether in my career, relationships, or personal endeavors, I felt a constant need to be flawless. Any mistake or shortcoming was a source of intense self-criticism. The pursuit of perfection became a relentless cycle, one that left little room for self-compassion or growth.

It was during a pivotal moment in my career that I truly confronted this burden. I had taken on a major project, one that was both ambitious and fraught with potential pitfalls. The stakes were high, and the pressure to succeed was immense. I poured all my energy into it, working long hours, sacrificing sleep, and neglecting my well-being.

Despite my best efforts, the project encountered unforeseen challenges. There were delays, setbacks, and moments of sheer frustration. As the deadline approached, the weight of expectations became almost unbearable. I felt like I was carrying the world on my shoulders, and any misstep would lead to disaster.

One evening, after a particularly grueling day, I found myself standing in front of the mirror, staring at my reflection. The person looking back at me was exhausted, drained of energy and spirit. It was at that moment that I realized something had to change. The pursuit of perfection was not only unsustainable but also detrimental to my mental and physical health.

I made a conscious decision to let go of the need to be perfect. Instead, I focused on doing my best, embracing the process, and learning from my mistakes. It was a difficult shift, one that required constant reminders and self-reflection. But gradually, I began to see the benefits.

By releasing the unrealistic expectations, I found a sense of freedom. I allowed myself to be human, to make errors, and to grow from them. This shift in mindset not only improved my work but also enhanced my overall well-being. I became more resilient, better equipped to handle challenges, and more compassionate toward myself and others.

The weight of expectations also permeated my personal life. There was the expectation to maintain certain relationships, to meet societal standards of success, and to conform to roles that didn't always align with my true self. Breaking free from these expectations required a deep exploration of my values and desires.

I began to prioritize what truly mattered to me, rather than what was expected of me. This involved setting boundaries, saying no when necessary, and being honest about my needs and limitations. It was a process of redefining success on my terms, finding joy in the present, and embracing the imperfect journey.

One of the most significant changes was how I approached relationships. The expectation to be everything to everyone had left me feeling stretched thin and disconnected. I realized that true connection required authenticity, vulnerability, and mutual respect. By being honest about my struggles and listening to the struggles of others, I forged deeper, more meaningful bonds.

Family dynamics were another area where the weight of expectations loomed large. The desire to live up to parental expectations, to be the ideal child, sibling, or partner, often created tension and misunderstandings. Open communication and setting realistic expectations became crucial. Through heartfelt conversations, I found that my loved ones, too, were carrying their burdens of expectation. Together, we worked toward a more supportive and understanding dynamic.

As I navigated this journey, I discovered that expectations, when balanced with self-awareness and compassion, could be powerful motivators. They pushed me to strive for excellence, to dream big, and to pursue my passions. But it was equally important to recognize the limits, to know when to push and when to step back.

The process of managing expectations, both external and internal, is ongoing. It requires constant reflection, adjustment, and a willingness to be kind to oneself. Through this journey, I've learned that resilience is not about being unbreakable; it's about bending, adapting, and finding strength in vulnerability.

I remember a specific instance that encapsulated this journey. I was invited to speak at a significant conference, an opportunity I had long aspired to. The expectation to deliver a flawless presentation weighed heavily on me. I spent countless hours preparing, revising, and practicing. Despite my efforts, as the day approached, anxiety gripped me. I feared not meeting the high expectations I had set for myself.

On the day of the conference, standing backstage, I felt the familiar pangs of doubt and fear. But I reminded myself of the lessons learned. Instead of striving for perfection, I focused on authenticity—sharing my true self and experiences with the audience. As I stepped onto the stage, I took a deep breath, let go of the need for perfection, and spoke from the heart.

The response was overwhelming. The audience connected with my vulnerability, my honesty, and the genuine message I conveyed. It was a powerful reminder that authenticity resonates far more than a polished façade. The experience reinforced the importance of being true to oneself, embracing imperfections, and finding strength in vulnerability.

As the sun set over the city, casting a golden glow on the horizon, I felt a sense of peace. The journey ahead remained uncertain, but I was equipped with the tools and insights to navigate it with grace. With each chapter yet unwritten, I embraced the promise of tomorrow, ready to face the challenges and opportunities that lay ahead. The weight of expectations, once a heavy burden, had become a source of strength, propelling me toward a future filled with hope, resilience, and endless possibilities.

FINDING STRENGTH IN VULNERABILITY

The notion of vulnerability often carries a negative connotation, evoking images of weakness and exposure. Yet, as I navigated through the trials and tribulations of my journey, I discovered that true strength lies in embracing vulnerability. It is in our most vulnerable moments that we find our deepest reservoirs of courage, resilience, and authenticity. Vulnerability was not something I had readily embraced. For much of my life, I had built walls around myself, believing that showing any sign of weakness would leave me open to hurt and disappointment.

These walls, while providing a semblance of protection, also kept me isolated and disconnected from others and, ultimately, from myself. One of the pivotal moments in my journey came when I decided to seek therapy. It was a decision born out of desperation, as the weight of my past traumas and unresolved emotions had become too much to bear alone. Walking into that therapist's office for the first time, I felt a mixture of fear and relief. I was about to expose the deepest, most painful parts of myself to a stranger, and the thought was terrifying.

Yet, as I began to open up, sharing my fears, regrets, and long-buried memories, I felt a sense of liberation. The therapist's compassionate, nonjudgmental presence provided a safe space for me to confront my vulnerabilities. Through our sessions, I started to understand that vulnerability was not a sign of weakness, but a path to healing and self-acceptance.

I recall a particular session where I spoke about a significant loss from my past. It was an experience that had left a profound scar, one that I had tried to ignore and suppress for years. As I recounted the events, tears flowed freely, and for the first time, I allowed myself to fully feel the pain and grief.

The therapist encouraged me to sit with these emotions, to acknowledge them rather than push them away. At that moment, I realized that by embracing my vulnerability, I was also embracing my humanity. The pain, the sorrow, and the tears were all part of my story, and by acknowledging them, I was reclaiming my power.

This process of vulnerability and acceptance was not easy, but it was transformative. It opened the door to deeper self-understanding and compassion, both for myself and for others.

Outside of therapy, I began to practice vulnerability in my daily life. This meant being honest about my feelings, asking for help when I needed it, and allowing myself to be seen for who I truly was. It was a gradual process, filled with moments of discomfort and self-doubt, but each step brought me closer to a more authentic existence.

One of the areas where vulnerability had the most profound impact was in my relationships. For years, I had kept my true self hidden, presenting a façade that I believed would protect me from rejection and judgment. This façade, however, also kept me from forming deep, meaningful connections.

As I started to lower my defenses, I noticed a shift in my relationships. By being open about my struggles and fears, I created space for genuine connection. Friends and loved ones responded with empathy and understanding, and our bonds grew stronger.

Vulnerability became a bridge, connecting me to others in ways I had never experienced before. A particularly memorable instance was a conversation with a close friend. We had known each other for years, but there was always a sense of guardedness in our interactions.

One evening, I decided to share some of the personal challenges I was facing. To my surprise, my friend responded by opening up about her struggles. In that moment of mutual vulnerability, we found a deeper connection—one that was based on honesty and trust.

Another area where vulnerability played a crucial role was in my creative pursuits. As a writer, I had often struggled with self-doubt and fear of criticism. I hesitated to share my work, worried that it would not be good enough. But as I embraced vulnerability, I found the courage to put my true self into my writing.

"Sharing my stories, thoughts, and emotions through my writing became an act of vulnerability."

It was a way of saying, "This is who I am, with all my imperfections and flaws." The response was overwhelmingly positive.

Readers connected with the authenticity of my work, and I received messages from people who found solace and inspiration in my words.

This feedback reinforced the power of vulnerability in creating a meaningful impact.

As I continued to embrace vulnerability, I also learned to be gentle with myself. The journey of self-discovery and healing was not linear; it was filled with ups and downs, moments of clarity, and moments of confusion.

There were times when I fell back into old patterns of self-protection and fear. But each time, I reminded myself that "vulnerability" was a practice, one that required patience and perseverance.

The lessons I learned about vulnerability extended beyond personal growth. They influenced how I approached my professional life, my interactions with others, and my overall perspective on life. I began to see vulnerability as a strength, a source of resilience that allowed me to face challenges with courage and authenticity.

In my professional life, embracing vulnerability meant being open to feedback, acknowledging my mistakes, and seeking collaboration. It fostered an environment of trust and mutual respect, where ideas could flourish, and innovation could thrive.

By leading with vulnerability, I encouraged others to do the same, creating a culture of openness and growth.

Reflecting on my journey, I realized that vulnerability was the key to unlocking my true potential. It allowed me to connect with my deepest self, build authentic relationships, and live a life that was true to my values and passions. The path of vulnerability was not without its challenges, but it was a path worth taking.

As I stood on the cusp of new beginnings, I carried the lessons of vulnerability with me. They were a reminder that true strength comes from embracing our imperfections, from daring to be seen, and from opening our hearts to the world.

The echoes of resilience, shaped by vulnerability, continued to guide me, illuminating the path ahead with hope and courage.

One of the most significant moments of embracing vulnerability came when I decided to share my story publicly. I had been writing privately for years, documenting my experiences and reflections, but the thought of sharing these intimate details with the world was daunting.

Yet, I felt a compelling urge to do so, believing that my story could help others who were on their journeys of resilience and healing.

I decided to start a blog, "True Thoughts and Emotions," a platform where I could share my thoughts, experiences, and lessons learned. The first post was the hardest.

I spent days drafting and redrafting, doubting myself at every turn. But finally, I hit "publish," and with that single act, I opened myself up to the world.

The response was incredible. People from all walks of life reached out, sharing their own stories of struggle and triumph. They expressed gratitude for my honesty and courage, and many said that my words had touched them deeply.

The sense of connection and community that emerged was profoundly moving. It reaffirmed my belief that vulnerability fosters genuine human connections.

As my blog gained traction, I received invitations to speak at events and workshops. Public speaking was another area where I had to confront my fears and embrace vulnerability. Standing in front of an audience, sharing personal stories and insights, was both terrifying and exhilarating.

But each time I spoke, I felt a little more confident, a little more assured in the power of my voice.

Through these experiences, I learned that vulnerability is a gift we give to ourselves and others. It allows us to be seen for who we truly are, fostering deeper connections and mutual understanding.

It also encourages others to embrace their vulnerabilities, creating a ripple effect of authenticity and empathy.

In my personal life, the practice of vulnerability continued to strengthen my relationships. I found that by being open and honest, I was able to build deeper, more meaningful connections.

This was especially true in my romantic relationships. By sharing my fears, insecurities, and dreams, I created a space for genuine intimacy and trust.

One evening, while having a heartfelt conversation with my partner, I realized just how far I had come. We talked about our hopes and fears, our past experiences, and our visions for the future.

It was a moment of profound connection, one that would not have been possible without the willingness to be vulnerable. At that moment, I felt a deep sense of gratitude for the journey I had undertaken and for the strength I had found in my vulnerability.

As I continued to navigate life's twists and turns, I carried the lessons of vulnerability with me. They became a guiding principle, a source of resilience in times of uncertainty.

Whether facing new challenges, building relationships, or pursuing my passions, I knew that embracing vulnerability would always lead me to a place of deeper understanding and growth.

The journey was far from over, but with each step, I felt more grounded and more connected to myself and others. The echoes of resilience, shaped by my experiences and reflections, continued to guide me, illuminating the path ahead.

As I moved forward, I embraced the unknown with an open heart, ready to face whatever came my way with courage, authenticity, and unwavering resilience. In the end, the greatest lesson I learned was that true strength comes from embracing our vulnerabilities, from daring to be seen, and from opening our hearts to the world.

This journey, with all its trials and triumphs, taught me that resilience is not about being invincible, but about being real. And in that realness, I found the strength to keep moving forward, to keep growing, and to keep living a life true to myself.

The echoes of resilience, shaped by the vulnerability I embraced, became a powerful force in my life. They reminded me that I was capable of facing any challenge, overcoming any obstacle, and continuing on my path with unwavering determination.

Through the practice of vulnerability, I found a deeper connection to myself and the world around me. And in that connection, I discovered the true essence of resilience.

Embracing the Uncertainty

The future is a blank canvas, full of potential but also laden with uncertainty. For many, including myself, the unknown can be a source of anxiety and fear. However, my journey has taught me that within this uncertainty lies the possibility of growth and transformation.

Embracing uncertainty meant letting go of the need to control every aspect of my life. It required a shift in mindset, from seeing uncertainty as a threat to viewing it as an opportunity. This change was neither quick nor easy, but it was essential for my continued growth.

One of the most significant steps in embracing uncertainty came when I decided to pursue a passion project that had always lingered in the back of my mind. It was an idea I had toyed with for years but had never dared to take seriously due to the fear of failure and the comfort of stability. But the lessons of resilience and vulnerability had given me the courage to take that leap.

I remember the moment vividly. I was sitting at my desk, staring at the familiar environment of my job and feeling a profound sense of unfulfillment. The work was secure, and the paycheck was steady, but it lacked meaning and passion.

I decided then that it was time to take a risk, embrace the uncertainty, and pursue something that truly resonated with my heart.

The transition was not smooth. It involved leaving a stable job, facing financial uncertainties, and stepping into a field where success was not guaranteed. But each step, though fraught with challenges, brought me closer to a sense of purpose and fulfillment that I had long been missing.

One of the first projects I embarked on was creating a community initiative that aimed to support individuals dealing with loss and grief. Drawing from my own experiences, I wanted to create a space where people could find solace, share their stories, and build resilience together.

It was a deeply personal project, one that required me to be vulnerable and open about my journey. Launching the initiative was a daunting task. There were moments of doubt, sleepless nights, and setbacks that made me question whether I had made the right choice. But through it all, the echoes of resilience kept me going.

The support and feedback from the community were overwhelming. People shared their gratitude for the space, their stories of loss and recovery, and their appreciation for the connections they were able to make.

As the initiative grew, I realized that embracing uncertainty had opened doors I never knew existed. It allowed me to create something meaningful, to touch lives in ways I had never imagined.

The fear of the unknown had been replaced by the excitement of potential and the joy of making a difference.

In my personal life, embracing uncertainty also meant being open to new experiences and relationships. It involved letting go of rigid plans and expectations, allowing life to unfold in its own time.

This approach brought a sense of freedom and spontaneity that had been missing from my life.

I started to travel more, exploring places I had always wanted to visit but had put off due to the demands of work and routine. These travels were not just physical journeys but also journeys of self-discovery. Each new place, with its unique culture and people, offered lessons and perspectives that enriched my understanding of the world and myself.

One memorable trip was to a small village in the mountains, far removed from the hustle and bustle of city life. The simplicity and beauty of the place were a stark contrast to my usual environment.

There, I found a sense of peace and clarity that I had been seeking. The villagers, with their warm hospitality and simple way of life, taught me the value of slowing down, of appreciating the present moment.

These experiences reinforced the idea that uncertainty is not something to be feared but embraced. It is in the unknown that we find the growth potential, the opportunity for new experiences, and the chance to discover aspects of ourselves that we never knew existed.

As I continued to embrace uncertainty, I also learned the importance of being present. The future, with all its unknowns, can often overshadow the present moment. But by focusing on the here and now, I found a sense of grounding and peace.

Mindfulness practices, such as meditation and journaling, became essential tools in my journey, helping me stay centered amidst the unpredictability of life.

Reflecting on my journey, I realized that the path of resilience and vulnerability had prepared me for the uncertainties of the future. It equipped me with the tools to navigate the unknown with grace and courage.

The echoes of resilience, born from my experiences and reflections, continued to guide me, reminding me that I was capable of facing whatever came my way.

Embracing uncertainty had become a way of life, a mindset that allowed me to approach each day with an open heart and a spirit of adventure. It taught me that life's greatest rewards often come from stepping out of our comfort zones, from daring to explore the unknown.

The journey was far from over, but with each step, I felt more confident, more resilient, and more alive. The echoes of resilience, shaped by my willingness to embrace vulnerability and uncertainty, became a powerful force, guiding me toward a future filled with endless possibilities. And with that, I continued on my path, ready to face whatever lay ahead, knowing that within the uncertainty lay the promise of growth and transformation.

As I moved forward, I embraced each new day as an opportunity to grow and learn. Embracing uncertainty fundamentally changed my outlook on life, transforming fear into curiosity and doubt into determination.

The journey was not without its challenges, but with every step, I felt more equipped to face whatever came my way.

The Power of Connection

In the wake of embracing uncertainty, I discovered another profound truth: the importance of human connection. While my journey had been deeply personal, it was the relationships I formed along the way that provided strength, support, and a sense of belonging.

One of the most significant connections I made was through my blog, "True Thoughts and Emotions." What began as a personal outlet for my reflections soon grew into a community of like-minded individuals who found solace and inspiration in my words.

"Sharing my vulnerabilities and experiences resonated with readers from all walks of life, creating a network of support and empathy."

Through the blog, I received messages from people who were navigating their journeys of resilience.

Their stories were diverse, yet the common thread was the human capacity to endure and grow despite adversity.

These connections enriched my understanding of resilience and highlighted the collective strength found in shared experiences.

One memorable interaction was with a reader named Sarah. She had been following my blog for months and reached out to share her story. Sarah had faced numerous challenges, from losing her job to battling a serious illness.

Despite these hardships, she found strength in her resilience and the support of her loved ones. Our correspondence became a source of mutual encouragement, reminding us both of the power of connection.

Inspired by these interactions, I decided to create a series of workshops and meetups centered around the themes of resilience, vulnerability, and personal growth.

These gatherings provided a space for individuals to share their stories, learn from one another, and build a supportive community.

The response was overwhelmingly positive, reinforcing the idea that we are stronger together than we are alone.

During one of the workshops, I met James, a man who had recently retired and was struggling to find purpose in his new phase of life. James shared how he felt adrift, his days lacking the structure and meaning that his career had once provided.

Together, we explored ways to rediscover passion and fulfillment, and he eventually found joy in volunteering and mentoring others. These workshops not only helped others but also deepened my understanding of resilience.

Each story I heard, each connection I made, added to the tapestry of my journey. The collective wisdom and strength of the community became a wellspring of inspiration, reminding me that resilience is a shared journey.

Outside of the workshops, I also focused on strengthening my relationships. Reconnecting with family and old friends, I realized the importance of nurturing these bonds. The conversations, laughter, and shared memories brought a renewed sense of warmth and connection to my life.

One evening, I hosted a small gathering at my home, inviting close friends and family members. As we sat around the table, sharing stories and laughter, I felt an overwhelming sense of gratitude.

These were the people who had stood by me through thick and thin, who had believed in me even when I doubted myself. Their presence was a testament to the enduring power of love and connection.

In my professional life, I continued to seek out meaningful work that aligned with my values.

Collaborating with others who shared my passion for making a difference, I found a sense of camaraderie and purpose.

These professional connections were more than just colleagues; they were partners in the journey of creating positive change.

One project that stood out was a collaboration with a non-profit organization focused on mental health awareness.

Together, we developed programs to support individuals dealing with mental health challenges, providing resources, counseling, and community support. This work was deeply fulfilling, as it combined my passion for helping others with the skills I had developed over the years.

Through these connections, I learned that resilience is not a solitary endeavor. It is nurtured and strengthened by the relationships we build, the love we give and receive, and the support we offer one another.

In moments of doubt and difficulty, it was the people around me who lifted me, reminding me of my strength and potential.

As I reflected on this chapter of my journey, I felt a profound sense of interconnectedness.

The echoes of resilience were not just my own; they resonated through the lives of those I had touched and who had touched mine. Together, we created a symphony of strength, hope, and compassion.

The journey was far from over, but with each step, I felt more confident, more resilient, and more connected.

The power of human connection had become a cornerstone of my resilience, a reminder that we are never truly alone. And with that, I continued on my path, ready to face whatever lay ahead, knowing that with the support of my community, I could overcome any obstacle and embrace any challenge.

FINDING PURPOSE

As my journey progressed, I found myself increasingly drawn to the idea of purpose.

What did it mean to live a purposeful life?

How could I align my actions with my deepest values and passions?

These questions guided me as I sought to understand the true essence of fulfillment. The search for purpose often begins with introspection. I took time to reflect on my experiences, my dreams, and the moments that had brought me the most joy and meaning.

Through journaling and meditation, I uncovered patterns and themes that pointed toward my core passions: helping others, fostering connections, and creating positive change.

One of the most transformative realizations came during a quiet evening at home. I was reading through old entries in my blog, "True Thoughts and Emotions," and the comments from readers who had been touched by my words.

Their stories of resilience and growth reaffirmed the impact of sharing my journey. I realized that my purpose was not just about my healing but also about inspiring and supporting others on their paths.

With this newfound clarity, I decided to expand my efforts. The community initiative I had started grew into a full-fledged organization dedicated to promoting mental health and emotional well-being.

We offered workshops, support groups, and resources to help individuals navigate their challenges and build resilience. The organization became a beacon of hope for many, providing a safe space for healing and growth.

Working on this project brought a sense of fulfillment that I had never experienced before.

Every success and every story of transformation reinforced my belief in the power of purpose. I saw firsthand how aligning my work with my values created a ripple effect, touching the lives of countless individuals.

One of the most impactful programs we launched was a mentorship initiative for young adults. Many of them were struggling with the pressures of academic and career expectations, feeling lost and uncertain about their futures.

Through one-on-one mentoring, we provided guidance, support, and encouragement, helping them discover their passions and chart their paths.

One mentee, Emily, stood out. She had always dreamed of becoming an artist but felt pressured to pursue a more "practical" career. Through our sessions, she found the courage to follow her passion, eventually showcasing her work in local galleries. Her journey was a testament to the power of purpose and the importance of following one's true calling.

In my personal life, finding purpose also meant nurturing my relationships and investing in my well-being. I made time for activities that brought me joy, from hiking in nature to spending quality time with loved ones. These moments of connection and self-care were essential in maintaining my balance and sustaining my energy for the work I was passionate about.

One particularly meaningful experience was a retreat I attended focused on mindfulness and self-discovery. Surrounded by nature and like-minded individuals, I immersed myself in practices that deepened my understanding of purpose and presence. The retreat was a time of renewal and reflection, reinforcing the importance of staying connected to my inner self.

As I embraced my purpose, I also learned to be adaptable. Life is full of unexpected twists and turns, and purpose is not a fixed destination but a dynamic journey. There were times when I faced setbacks and challenges, but each obstacle became an opportunity to realign and refocus. The lessons of resilience and vulnerability remained my guiding principles, helping me navigate the uncertainties with grace and determination.

The journey of finding purpose was not without its moments of doubt and fear. There were times when I questioned my path, wondering if I was making the right choices. But in those moments, I turned to the community I had built and the connections I had forged. Their support and encouragement reminded me of the impact I was making and the importance of staying true to my purpose.

As I continued to grow and evolve, so did my understanding of purpose. It was not a singular goal but a multifaceted expression of my values and passions. It encompassed my work, my relationships, and my personal growth. Purpose became a way of being, a lens through which I viewed and approached life.

Reflecting on this chapter of my journey, I felt a profound sense of gratitude for the path I had walked and the lessons I had learned. Finding purpose transformed my life, bringing meaning and fulfillment to each day. The echoes of resilience, shaped by my experiences and reflections, continued to guide me, illuminating the path ahead.

With a clear sense of purpose, I embraced the future with confidence and excitement. The journey was far from over, but with each step, I felt more aligned with my true self and more connected to the world around me. The power of purpose, intertwined with resilience and connection, became a driving force, guiding me toward a future filled with endless possibilities and profound fulfillment.

With an open heart and an unwavering spirit, I continued on my path, ready to face whatever lay ahead. The echoes of resilience and purpose resonated deeply within me, a constant reminder of the strength and potential that lay within each of us. And with that, I moved forward, embracing the journey and all it had to offer, knowing that I was exactly where I was meant to be toward the future with a renewed sense of hope and possibility.

Forgiveness allowed me to approach life with an open heart, unencumbered by the weight of past grievances. It created space for new experiences, relationships, and opportunities that aligned with my authentic self. As I embraced this newfound freedom, I discovered a deeper sense of fulfillment and a more profound connection to my purpose.

In the months following my commitment to forgiveness, I noticed how it influenced my interactions and decisions. I approached challenges with a greater sense of resilience, viewing them as opportunities for growth rather than obstacles. I was more willing to extend grace to others and myself, recognizing that we are all on a journey of learning and evolving.

One day, as I walked through a park, I observed the changes in nature around me. The trees were shedding their old leaves, making way for new growth. This natural process mirrored my own experience of letting go and embracing change. Just as the trees evolved with the seasons, I was learning to adapt and grow, shedding the past to make room for a more vibrant future.

Embracing forgiveness also meant re-evaluating my goals and aspirations. I began to pursue passions that aligned with my values and brought me genuine joy. I found fulfillment in mentoring others, engaging in creative projects, and advocating for causes I deeply cared about. These pursuits not only enriched my life but also reinforced my sense of purpose and connection.

One significant project I undertook was starting a community initiative focused on mental health and resilience. Drawing from my own experiences, I sought to create a space where individuals could share their stories, seek support, and find inspiration. The initiative was met with enthusiasm and support, and it became a testament to the power of collective healing and growth.

As I reflected on my journey, I realized that forgiveness had been a key catalyst for transformation. It liberated me from the confines of past hurts and allowed me to embrace a more authentic and fulfilling life. Each act of forgiveness, whether toward others or myself, was a step toward greater peace and resilience.

Looking ahead, I remained committed to the practice of forgiveness. I knew that life would continue to present challenges and moments of difficulty, but I also understood that forgiveness was a powerful tool for navigating them. It was a practice that required ongoing effort and reflection, but one that offered profound rewards in terms of personal growth and emotional well-being.

The echoes of resilience, now intertwined with the lessons of forgiveness, guided me with a sense of clarity and purpose. As I moved forward, I carried with me the understanding that true strength lies in the ability to let go of the past, embrace the present, and face the future with an open heart. With each step, I continued to build on the foundation of authenticity and forgiveness, embracing the opportunities and challenges that lay ahead.

And so, with gratitude and resolve, I faced the future with an unwavering spirit. The journey of forgiveness had transformed my life, and I welcomed each new day with a heart full of hope, ready to embrace the endless possibilities that awaited.

Embracing Authenticity

As I journeyed further along my path, I came to realize that one of the most critical components of resilience and fulfillment was embracing authenticity. Authenticity required me to be true to myself, to honor my values, beliefs, and unique experiences, and to let go of societal expectations and pressures that didn't align with my true self.

The journey to authenticity began with a deep, often uncomfortable, self-exploration. I needed to confront the parts of myself I had long hidden or suppressed out of fear of judgment or rejection. This process was both liberating and daunting, requiring me to strip away layers of pretense and reveal my true self, imperfections and all.

One of the first steps in embracing authenticity was acknowledging and accepting my past. My experiences, both positive and negative, had shaped who I was. The trials and tribulations, the relationships and losses, the successes and failures—all of these elements were integral to my story. By accepting them without shame or regret, I could begin to understand and embrace the person I had become.

I recalled a significant moment of self-acceptance that occurred during a speaking engagement. I had been invited to share my story at a conference on mental health and resilience. Standing on stage, I felt a familiar wave of anxiety wash over me. But instead of succumbing to it, I decided to speak from the heart, without a script, sharing my journey with raw honesty.

As I spoke, I could feel the room's energy shift. My vulnerability resonated with the audience, and I saw nods of understanding and empathy. When I finished, the applause was overwhelming but more meaningful were the conversations that followed. People approached me to share their own stories, struggles, and triumphs. It was a powerful reminder that authenticity fosters connection and compassion.

In my personal life, embracing authenticity meant being honest with myself and others about my needs, boundaries, and desires. I learned to say no to things that didn't align with my values and to prioritize what truly mattered to me. This shift wasn't always easy; it meant making difficult choices and sometimes disappointing others.

But it also brought a profound sense of freedom and integrity.

One of the most challenging aspects of authenticity was addressing the societal pressures and expectations that had influenced my life. From a young age, I had been conditioned to seek approval and validation from external sources—whether through academic achievements, career success, or social acceptance. Letting go of these external markers and defining success on my terms was a radical act of self-liberation.

A turning point came when I decided to downsize my lifestyle. I had been living in a spacious apartment in a bustling city, surrounded by the trappings of success. But deep down, I felt disconnected from the person I was becoming. I realized that material possessions and social status were not true indicators of fulfillment. With this in mind,

I moved to a smaller, simpler home in a quieter neighborhood. This decision allowed me to focus on what truly brought me joy and peace—nature, creativity, and meaningful connections.

In my professional life, embracing authenticity led me to reassess my career goals. I shifted my focus from climbing the corporate ladder to pursuing work that aligned with my passions and values. This transition wasn't without its challenges, but it was deeply rewarding. I found myself more engaged and fulfilled, surrounded by colleagues who shared my commitment to making a positive impact.

Authenticity also transformed my relationships. By being open and honest about who I was and what I needed, I formed deeper, more genuine connections with others. I no longer felt the need to conform to others' expectations or hide my true self. This authenticity fostered mutual respect and understanding, creating a foundation for lasting, meaningful relationships.

One of the most profound realizations was that authenticity is an ongoing journey, not a destination. It requires continuous self-reflection and a willingness to evolve. There were moments of doubt and setbacks, times when I questioned whether I was being true to myself. But each challenge was an opportunity to reaffirm my commitment to living authentically.

As I embraced authenticity, I noticed a shift in my overall well-being. I felt more at peace with myself, more connected to others, and more aligned with my purpose. The echoes of resilience, shaped by my journey of self-discovery, became a guiding force, reminding me of the strength and potential that lay within me.

Reflecting on this chapter of my journey, I felt a deep sense of gratitude for the lessons learned and the growth achieved. Embracing authenticity has transformed my life, bringing clarity, fulfillment, and a profound sense of self-worth. The journey was far from over, but with each step, I felt more confident and empowered to face whatever lay ahead.

And so, with an open heart and an unwavering commitment to authenticity, I continued on my path. The echoes of resilience and authenticity resonated deeply within me, guiding me toward a future filled with endless possibilities and profound fulfillment. Embracing my true self, I welcomed the challenges and opportunities that lay ahead, ready to live each day with integrity, purpose, and a deep sense of connection to myself and the world around me.

THE POWER OF FORGIVENESS

The next stage of my journey led me to a place I had often avoided: forgiveness. Forgiveness, both for others and for myself, was an essential part of healing and growth. It required me to confront old wounds, let go of lingering resentments, and embrace the freedom that comes from releasing the past.

Forgiving others was not an easy task. It meant revisiting painful memories and facing the emotions I had long buried. But I realized that holding onto anger and bitterness was like carrying a heavy burden, one that weighed me down and hindered my progress. By choosing to forgive, I was not excusing the actions that had hurt me, but rather freeing myself from their grip.

One of the most challenging relationships to navigate was with a close friend who had betrayed my trust. The betrayal had left a deep scar, and for years, I carried the hurt and resentment. But as I embarked on my journey of self-discovery and healing, I understood that holding onto these feelings was preventing me from fully moving forward.

I decided to reach out to this friend, not necessarily to rekindle the friendship, but to find closure and peace. Our conversation was difficult, filled with raw honesty and vulnerability. Through tears and heartfelt words, we acknowledged the pain and the impact it had on both of us. At that moment, I felt a weight lift from my shoulders.

Forgiveness was not about forgetting or minimizing the hurt; it was about reclaiming my power and choosing to move forward with a lighter heart.

Forgiving myself was perhaps the hardest part of this journey. I had been my harshest critic, often dwelling on my mistakes and perceived failures. But self-forgiveness was crucial for my growth and well-being. It meant accepting my imperfections, acknowledging my humanity, and giving myself the grace to learn and evolve.

I remember a particularly poignant moment during a meditation retreat. We were guided through a practice of self-compassion, where we silently repeated phrases of kindness and forgiveness to ourselves.

As I sat in the quiet room, surrounded by others on their journeys, I felt a deep sense of release. I forgave myself for the choices I regretted, the times I had fallen short, and the moments of weakness. In that space of acceptance, I found a profound sense of peace and self-love.

Forgiveness also extended to the societal and cultural influences that had shaped my beliefs and behaviors. Growing up, I had internalized many messages about success, worth, and identity. Letting go of these ingrained notions was a form of forgiveness, allowing me to redefine my values and live authentically.

As I embraced forgiveness, I noticed a transformation in my relationships. Letting go of past grievances made space for compassion and understanding. I found myself more patient and empathetic, able to see others through the lens of their struggles and growth. This shift deepened my connections and fostered a sense of unity and shared humanity.

One significant experience was a reconciliation with a family member with whom I had a long-standing conflict. The tension had strained our relationship for years, but as I committed to forgiveness, I reached out with an open heart. Our initial conversations were cautious, but over time, we began to rebuild trust and understanding.

This healing process strengthened our bond and brought a sense of harmony to our family.

Through this journey, I learned that forgiveness is a continuous practice, not a one-time act. There were moments when old wounds resurfaced, and the feelings of hurt and anger reappeared. But each time, I reminded myself of the liberation that comes with forgiveness and chose to release the past once more. This ongoing practice reinforced my resilience and allowed me to face challenges with a clearer, more compassionate perspective.

Reflecting on this chapter, I felt immense gratitude for the lessons of forgiveness. It transformed my life, bringing peace, healing, and a deeper understanding of myself and others. The echoes of resilience, intertwined with forgiveness, became a guiding force, illuminating my path and strengthening my spirit.

As I continued my journey, I embraced the power of forgiveness, knowing it was a vital part of living authentically and purposefully. The past, with all its trials and tribulations, had shaped me, but it no longer defined me. With a heart unburdened by resentment, I looked

Cultivating Inner Peace

With forgiveness paving the way for a more authentic and fulfilling life, I turned my attention to cultivating inner peace. Inner peace was the foundation upon which I could build a resilient and purposeful existence. It was about finding tranquility amidst the chaos and developing a sense of calm that transcended external circumstances.

The quest for inner peace began with creating space for stillness and reflection. In the past, I had often been caught in the whirlwind of daily responsibilities, leaving little time for introspection. However, I realized that to cultivate inner peace, I needed to make intentional space for quiet moments of self-reflection and mindfulness.

I started incorporating meditation into my daily routine. Each morning, I would sit in a quiet corner of my home, close my eyes, and focus on my breath. The initial practice was challenging; my mind was flooded with distractions and racing thoughts. But with persistence, I began to experience moments of deep calm and clarity.

Meditation became a sanctuary, a place where I could retreat from the noise of the world and reconnect with my inner self.

In addition to meditation, I explored other practices that contributed to my sense of inner peace. Journaling became a powerful tool for processing my thoughts and emotions. By writing regularly, I was able to articulate my feelings, gain insights into my patterns, and release pent-up stress. Journaling provided a way to navigate my internal landscape and foster self-awareness.

Spending time in nature also played a significant role in cultivating inner peace. I would often take walks in the park, allowing the natural beauty to soothe my mind and spirit. The rhythmic sounds of birdsong, the rustling of leaves, and the gentle breeze created a calming environment that helped me center myself.

Nature had a way of grounding me, reminding me of the simplicity and tranquility that existed beyond the hustle of daily life.

Building inner peace also required addressing the sources of stress and negativity in my life. I took a closer look at my relationships, work environment, and personal habits. I realized that certain relationships were draining my energy and contributing to my stress. It became necessary to set boundaries and distance myself from toxic influences.

This process was not always easy, but it was essential for preserving my mental and emotional well-being.

I also examined my work-life balance. The demands of my career had previously left me feeling overwhelmed and depleted. I began to reassess my priorities and make adjustments to ensure that work did not consume all of my time and energy. I sought out activities that brought me joy and fulfillment outside of work, allowing me to cultivate a more balanced and harmonious life.

Embracing self-compassion was another crucial aspect of cultivating inner peace. I learned to treat myself with kindness and understanding, especially during times of difficulty or self-doubt.

Instead of criticizing myself for perceived shortcomings, I practiced self-acceptance and encouraged a nurturing inner dialogue. This shift in perspective helped me maintain a sense of calm and resilience in the face of challenges.

As I continued on this path, I found that inner peace was not a static state but a dynamic process. It required ongoing attention and care, as well as a willingness to adapt and grow. There were moments when external circumstances tested my sense of tranquility, but I learned to approach these challenges with equanimity and grace. By grounding myself in the practices that fostered inner peace, I was better equipped to navigate life's ups and downs with a sense of calm and balance.

Reflecting on this chapter of my journey, I felt a deep sense of contentment and fulfillment. Cultivating inner peace transformed my outlook on life, providing a stable foundation from which to face challenges and embrace opportunities. It was a continuous practice, one that required dedication and mindfulness, but it offered profound rewards in terms of emotional resilience and well-being.

As I looked ahead, I remained committed to nurturing my inner peace. I knew that life would continue to present its share of trials and uncertainties, but I felt equipped to meet them with a sense of calm and composure. The echoes of resilience, now harmonized with inner peace, guided me with a profound sense of clarity and purpose.

Referred With each new day, I embraced the journey of cultivating inner peace, welcoming the opportunities for growth and self-discovery that lay ahead. The path was illuminated by a sense of tranquility and balance, and I continued to move forward with an open heart and a steadfast spirit, ready to face whatever the future held with grace and resilience

Embracing Change

As I continued to nurture inner peace, I realized that embracing change was a crucial part of my journey. Change, though often accompanied by uncertainty and discomfort, was an inevitable and necessary aspect of growth. It was through embracing change that I could continue evolving and adapting to the ever-shifting landscape of life.

The first step in embracing change was to shift my mindset from resistance to acceptance. I had spent much of my life clinging to familiarity and predictability, fearing the unknown and resisting alterations to my plans and routines. However, I came to understand that change was not something to be feared but rather an opportunity for growth and transformation.

One significant change in my life was the decision to leave a secure but unfulfilling job. For years, I had been entrenched in a corporate role that provided financial stability but lacked personal fulfillment. The decision to leave was not easy; it meant stepping away from a familiar path and venturing into the unknown.

Yet, I recognized that staying in a situation that no longer aligned with my values was a form of stagnation.

I spent time reflecting on my passions and interests, exploring potential career paths that resonated with my sense of purpose. This exploration was both exciting and daunting. It involved uncertainty and the possibility of failure, but it also held the promise of new opportunities and growth.

Eventually, I transitioned into a role that aligned more closely with my values and aspirations. The process of change was challenging, and filled with moments of self-doubt and adjustment. Yet, as

I settled into my new role, I found a renewed sense of purpose and fulfillment. The change pushed me out of my comfort zone and led to unexpected rewards.

Embracing change also involved adapting to shifts in personal relationships. As I grew and evolved, I noticed that some relationships naturally drifted apart, while others deepened and flourished. I learned to accept these dynamics with grace, understanding that change in relationships was a natural part of life.

One particular relationship that transformed me was with a long-time friend. As we both embarked on different life paths, our connection faced challenges. However, rather than letting the distance create a rift, we made a conscious effort to stay connected and support each other. Our relationship evolved into a new form, one that acknowledged the changes in our lives while preserving the essence of our bond.

I also encountered changes in my habits and routines. As I prioritized self-care and well-being, I experimented with new practices and activities that contributed to my growth. This included adopting healthier lifestyle choices, exploring new hobbies, and engaging in creative pursuits. Each change brought its own set of challenges, but it also offered opportunities for self-discovery and enrichment.

One significant change was the decision to relocate to a new city. The move represented a fresh start and an opportunity to immerse myself in a new environment. While it was initially overwhelming to leave behind the familiar, I embraced the adventure with an open mind and heart. The relocation brought new experiences, people, and perspectives, enriching my life in ways I had not anticipated.

As I navigated these changes, I learned to embrace flexibility and adaptability. Change often required me to let go of preconceived notions and expectations, and to remain open to the possibilities that emerged. It was a continual process of adjusting and recalibrating, but it led to a more dynamic and fulfilling life.

Reflecting on this chapter, I felt a deep sense of gratitude for the lessons learned through embracing change. It taught me resilience, adaptability, and the importance of remaining open to new experiences. The echoes of resilience, now intertwined with my acceptance of change, guided me with a renewed sense of purpose and possibility.

As I moved forward, I carried with me the understanding that change was an integral part of the journey. Each shift and transformation was a step toward growth and self-discovery. With an open heart and a willingness to embrace the unknown, I looked ahead with anticipation, ready to welcome the opportunities and challenges that lay in store.

The journey of embracing change was ongoing, and I remained committed to navigating it with grace and courage. The path ahead was illuminated by the lessons of resilience and acceptance, and I continued to move forward with a sense of excitement and optimism, eager to explore the endless possibilities that awaited.

FINDING JOY IN THE PRESENT MOMENT

Having learned to embrace change and cultivate inner peace, I realized that one of the most vital aspects of my journey was finding joy in the present moment. Too often, I had been caught up in worries about the future or regrets about the past, missing out on the simple pleasures and profound contentment that the present had to offer.

The practice of mindfulness became central to my quest for present-moment joy. Mindfulness was about fully engaging with the here and now, appreciating each experience without judgment or distraction. It was a skill that required practice and intention, but its benefits were transformative.

I began incorporating mindfulness into my daily life through various practices. Each morning, I would start my day with a few moments of mindful breathing, setting a positive and focused tone for the hours ahead. Throughout the day, I made a conscious effort to bring my attention back to the present, whether I was working, walking, or simply enjoying a meal. By focusing on my senses—the sights, sounds, smells, and textures around me—I cultivated a deeper connection to the present moment.

One of the most powerful experiences of present-moment joy came from my interactions with nature. I spent more time outdoors, whether in parks, gardens, or hiking trails. The natural world, with its intricate beauty and rhythmic cycles, provided endless opportunities for mindfulness. I found joy in the colors of a sunset, the rustle of leaves in the wind, and the simple act of walking barefoot on grass.

Nature's presence reminded me of the richness and wonder that existed in every moment.

Relationships also became a source of present-moment joy. I made an effort to be fully present with my loved ones, whether we were having a deep conversation or sharing a laugh over a cup of coffee. I listened with greater attentiveness, engaged with genuine curiosity, and cherished the time spent together. These moments of connection brought a profound sense of fulfillment and happiness.

Mindful activities such as cooking, reading, and creative pursuits became cherished rituals. I took pleasure in the process rather than rushing to the outcome. Cooking a meal became an act of love and creativity, reading a book became an immersive experience, and creating art became a meditative practice. These activities, when approached with mindfulness, enriched my life and brought a sense of calm and joy.

Practicing gratitude was another key element in finding joy in the present moment. Each day, I took a few moments to reflect on the things I was grateful for. This simple practice shifted my focus from what was lacking to what was abundant in my life. Gratitude opened my eyes to the small blessings and moments of beauty that I might have otherwise overlooked.

One evening, as I sat on my balcony watching the stars, I felt an overwhelming sense of peace and joy. The night was quiet, the air cool, and the sky was filled with countless twinkling lights. At that moment, I realized that joy was not something to be chased or achieved; it was something to be experienced right now, in the simplicity of the present.

Finding joy in the present moment did not mean ignoring life's challenges or denying difficult emotions. Instead, it was about embracing the full spectrum of human experience with openness and acceptance. It meant allowing myself to feel sadness, frustration, and uncertainty while also recognizing and savoring moments of joy and contentment.

As I reflected on this chapter of my journey, I felt a deep sense of contentment. Finding joy in the present moment has transformed my relationship with life, allowing me to live more fully and authentically. The echoes of resilience, now intertwined with mindfulness and gratitude, guided me with a sense of peace and purpose.

Looking ahead, I remained committed to the practice of present-moment joy. I knew that life would continue to present its share of challenges, but I also knew that joy could be found in even the smallest of moments. With each new day, I embraced the opportunity to live mindfully, appreciate the richness of the present, and to cultivate a sense of joy and gratitude.

The journey of finding joy in the present moment was ongoing, and I welcomed it with an open heart and a curious spirit. The path ahead was illuminated by the lessons of mindfulness and gratitude, and I continued to move forward with a sense of wonder and delight, eager to explore the endless possibilities that awaited in each moment.

The Power of Vulnerability

As I delved deeper into my journey, I came to understand the profound impact of vulnerability. For much of my life, I had viewed vulnerability as a weakness, something to be hidden or avoided. But through my experiences, I learned that vulnerability was, in fact, a powerful source of connection and strength.

The first step in embracing vulnerability was acknowledging my fears and insecurities. It meant facing the parts of myself that I had tried to conceal—my doubts, my failures, and my pain. This process was not easy. It required a level of honesty and self-compassion that I had not previously allowed myself. But as I began to peel back the layers of my defenses, I discovered a raw and authentic version of myself.

One of the most significant moments of vulnerability came when I decided to share my story on my blog, "True Thoughts and Emotions." Writing about my trials, tribulations, relationships, and losses was an act of courage. It meant exposing my innermost thoughts and experiences to the world and opening myself up to judgment and criticism. Yet, it was also an act of liberation. Sharing my story allowed me to connect with others who had faced similar struggles, creating a sense of community and mutual support.

The response to my blog was overwhelmingly positive. Readers reached out with messages of empathy and understanding, sharing their own stories of resilience and transformation. These connections were a testament to the power of vulnerability. By being open and honest about my journey, I had created a space where others felt safe to do the same.

Vulnerability also played a crucial role in my relationships. I learned that true intimacy and connection required a willingness to be vulnerable. This meant sharing my feelings and fears with my loved ones, even when it was uncomfortable. It meant allowing myself to be seen, not just in moments of strength but also in moments of weakness.

One of the most transformative experiences was a heart-to-heart conversation with a close friend. We had both been struggling with our challenges but had hesitated to share them out of fear of burdening each other. When we finally opened up, it was like a dam breaking. We shared our pain, our hopes, and our fears, and in doing so, we found a deeper level of connection and support. This conversation reinforced the idea that vulnerability was not a burden, but a bridge to deeper understanding and empathy.

In my professional life, I also embraced vulnerability by asking for help and admitting when I didn't have all the answers. This shift in approach fostered a more collaborative and supportive work environment. I found that colleagues were more willing to share their insights and struggles, leading to a more open and productive team dynamic.

One particular instance stood out. During a challenging project, I admitted to my team that I was feeling overwhelmed and unsure of the best approach. Rather than viewing this as a sign of weakness, my team rallied together, offering their support and ideas. This collective effort not only led to a successful outcome but also strengthened our bond as a team.

As I continued to embrace vulnerability, I noticed a profound shift in my sense of self. I felt more authentic, more connected, and more resilient. By allowing myself to be seen as I truly was—flaws and all—I experienced a deeper sense of self-acceptance and inner peace.

Reflecting on this chapter, I felt a deep sense of gratitude for the lessons learned through vulnerability. It taught me the importance of authenticity, connection, and empathy. The echoes of resilience, now intertwined with vulnerability, guided me with a renewed sense of strength and compassion.

Looking ahead, I remained committed to the practice of vulnerability. I knew that life would continue to present opportunities to be open and honest, and I welcomed them with an open heart. The journey of vulnerability was ongoing, and I embraced it with courage and humility, knowing that it was through vulnerability that I could continue to grow and connect with others.

The path ahead was illuminated by the lessons of vulnerability and resilience, and I continued to move forward with a sense of authenticity and openness, eager to explore the depths of connection and the power of being truly seen.

Embracing Imperfections

As my journey continued, I came to understand the importance of embracing imperfection. For much of my life, I had been a perfectionist, constantly striving to meet unrealistic standards and berating myself when I fell short. This relentless pursuit of perfection had taken a toll on my mental and emotional well-being, leaving me feeling exhausted and inadequate.

The first step in embracing imperfection was recognizing and challenging my perfectionistic tendencies. I realized that perfectionism was rooted in a fear of failure and a desire for approval. It was an attempt to control how others perceived me, to avoid criticism and rejection. But this constant striving for perfection was not sustainable, nor was it fulfilling.

I began to shift my mindset, focusing on progress rather than perfection. I allowed myself to make mistakes, to learn and grow from them, and to appreciate the journey rather than obsessing over the destination. This shift in perspective was liberating. It allowed me to let go of unrealistic expectations and to approach life with greater compassion and acceptance.

One of the most profound lessons in embracing imperfection came from my creative pursuits. Whether it was writing, painting, or cooking, I learned to appreciate the process rather than fixating on the result. I found joy in the act of creation, in experimenting and exploring, without the pressure of achieving a flawless outcome.

In my relationships, embracing imperfection meant accepting myself and others as we were, with all our flaws and imperfections. It meant recognizing that no one is perfect and that our imperfections are what make us human and relatable. This acceptance fostered deeper connections and greater empathy, allowing me to see the beauty in our shared humanity.

One particularly meaningful experience was a conversation with a friend who was struggling with self-doubt. She confided in me about her fears and insecurities, and in that moment, I realized how much I related to her feelings. I shared my struggles with perfectionism, and together, we supported and encouraged each other to embrace our imperfections. This mutual vulnerability and acceptance strengthened our friendship and reminded me of the power of authenticity.

In my professional life, embracing imperfection meant acknowledging that I didn't have to have all the answers or be the best at everything. It meant recognizing my strengths and weaknesses and being open to feedback and collaboration. This approach not only reduced my stress but also created a more supportive and innovative work environment.

One instance that stood out was a team project where I decided to delegate tasks and trust my colleagues' expertise. By acknowledging that I couldn't do everything perfectly on my own, I empowered my team to contribute their unique skills and perspectives. The result was a more dynamic and successful project and a reminder that collaboration often leads to better outcomes than striving for individual perfection.

As I continued to embrace imperfection, I noticed a profound shift in my sense of self-worth. I felt more at peace with myself, more accepting of my flaws, and more grateful for my strengths. I realized that imperfection was not a weakness, but a testament to my humanity and resilience.

Reflecting on this chapter, I felt a deep sense of gratitude for the lessons learned through embracing imperfection. It taught me the importance of self-compassion, authenticity, and connection. The echoes of resilience, now intertwined with acceptance and self-love, guided me with a renewed sense of confidence and contentment.

Looking ahead, I remained committed to the practice of embracing imperfection. I knew that life would continue to present challenges and opportunities for growth, and I welcomed them with an open heart. The journey of embracing imperfection was ongoing, and I approached it with curiosity and grace, knowing that it was through our imperfections that we found our true strength and beauty.

The path ahead was illuminated by the lessons of imperfection and resilience, and I continued to move forward with a sense of acceptance and joy, eager to explore the richness of life in all its imperfect glory.

The Art of Letting Go

As my journey unfolded, I came to understand the profound importance of letting go. Letting go of past hurts, rigid expectations, and the need for control was essential to my growth and well-being. This chapter of my life was about learning to release what no longer served me and to embrace the freedom and peace that came with letting go.

The first step in letting go was acknowledging the things I was holding on to. I realized that much of my emotional baggage was rooted in unresolved pain, unfulfilled expectations, and a fear of the unknown. Holding on to these things was a way of maintaining a sense of control, but it also kept me trapped in a cycle of suffering.

One of the most significant aspects of letting go was releasing past hurts and grievances. I had carried the weight of old wounds for far too long, allowing them to influence my present and future. It was time to forgive—not just others, but also myself. Forgiveness was not about condoning hurtful actions, but about freeing myself from the grip of resentment and pain.

I began a practice of writing letters to those who had hurt me, expressing my feelings, and then letting go. These letters were not meant to be sent; they were a way for me to process and release my emotions. As I wrote, I felt the weight of my grievances lift, replaced by a sense of peace and liberation. This practice also extended to forgiving myself for past mistakes and failures, allowing me to move forward with greater compassion and self-acceptance.

Letting go of rigid expectations was another crucial aspect of this journey. I had often set unrealistic standards for myself and others, leading to disappointment and frustration. By letting go of these expectations, I opened myself up to the possibilities of the present moment and allowed life to unfold naturally.

One poignant example was my career path. I had always envisioned a linear trajectory, with each step meticulously planned. But life had other plans. Unexpected changes and detours brought both challenges and opportunities. By letting go of my rigid expectations, I was able to embrace these changes with flexibility and openness, finding new paths that were more fulfilling and aligned with my true passions.

In my relationships, letting go meant releasing the need to control others and accepting them as they were. It meant allowing my loved ones to grow and change and supporting them in their journeys without imposing my expectations. This approach fostered deeper, more authentic connections, and allowed me to experience the beauty of unconditional love and acceptance.

The practice of mindfulness played a significant role in letting go. By staying present and aware, I was able to recognize when I was holding on to negative thoughts or emotions and to gently release them. Mindfulness helped me to stay grounded and centered, even in the face of uncertainty and change.

One evening, during a quiet meditation, I had a profound realization about the nature of control. I understood that true control was not about holding on tightly, but about trusting in the flow of life and adapting to its rhythms. This insight brought a deep sense of peace and acceptance, and I felt a renewed sense of trust in myself and the universe.

As I continued to practice letting go, I noticed a profound shift in my sense of well-being. I felt lighter, freer, and more at peace. Letting go had created space for new experiences, new connections, and new growth. It allowed me to move forward with a sense of clarity and purpose, unburdened by the weight of the past.

Reflecting on this chapter, I felt a deep sense of gratitude for the lessons learned through letting go. It taught me the importance of trust, acceptance, and freedom. The echoes of resilience, now intertwined with the art of letting go, guided me with a renewed sense of grace and ease.

Looking ahead, I remained committed to the practice of letting go. I knew that life would continue to present opportunities for release and renewal, and I welcomed them with an open heart. The journey of letting go was ongoing, and I approached it with curiosity and faith, knowing that it was through letting go that I could truly embrace the fullness of life.

The path ahead was illuminated by the lessons of letting go and resilience, and I continued to move forward with a sense of freedom and joy, eager to explore the boundless possibilities that awaited in the art of letting go.

THE HEALING POWER OF NATURE

Nature had always been a source of solace and inspiration for me, but it wasn't until I intentionally sought out its healing power that I truly understood its impact on my well-being. This chapter of my journey was about reconnecting with the natural world and discovering the profound sense of peace and renewal it offered.

The first step in this reconnection was simply spending more time outdoors. I made a conscious effort to incorporate nature into my daily routine, whether it was a morning walk in the park, an afternoon hike, or a weekend camping trip. These moments of immersion in nature allowed me to slow down, breathe deeply, and appreciate the beauty and simplicity of the natural world.

One particularly memorable experience was a solo camping trip I took to a remote forest. I had always enjoyed camping with friends and family, but this time, I felt the need to be alone with nature. The solitude and silence of the forest were initially daunting, but as the days passed, I felt a deep sense of peace and clarity. The sounds of the birds, the rustling of the leaves, and the sight of the star-filled sky at night brought a sense of wonder and connection that I had never felt before.

During this trip, I kept a journal, documenting my thoughts and reflections. I wrote about the healing power of nature, the way it seemed to wash away my worries and fill me with a sense of calm and presence. I realized that nature had a way of putting things into perspective, reminding me of the vastness and interconnectedness of life.

Back in the city, I sought out green spaces and natural settings whenever possible. I discovered local parks, botanical gardens, and nature reserves. These places became my sanctuaries, where I could retreat and recharge. I also started a small garden on my balcony, nurturing plants and flowers that brought a touch of nature into my daily life.

In addition to the physical benefits of being in nature, such as increased physical activity and exposure to sunlight, I found that nature had a profound impact on my mental and emotional health. It provided a sense of grounding and stability, a reminder of the rhythms and cycles of life. It taught me patience and resilience, as I observed the changing seasons and the delicate balance of ecosystems.

One of the most powerful lessons from nature was the concept of impermanence. I witnessed the constant ebb and flow of life, the way plants and animals adapted to changes, and the inevitability of growth and decay. This understanding helped me to accept the impermanence in my own life, to let go of attachments, and to embrace change with grace.

Nature also inspired creativity and mindfulness. I found that being in natural settings sparked new ideas and insights. I often brought a sketchbook or camera with me on my outings, capturing the beauty and details of the landscapes. These creative expressions were not about perfection, but about appreciating and celebrating the natural world.

As I continued to deepen my connection with nature, I felt a growing sense of stewardship and responsibility. I became more aware of environmental issues and the impact of human activities on the planet. This awareness motivated me to make more sustainable choices in my daily life, from reducing waste to supporting conservation efforts.

Reflecting on this chapter, I felt a deep sense of gratitude for the healing power of nature. It taught me the importance of presence, acceptance, and connection. The echoes of resilience, now intertwined with the wisdom of nature, guided me with a renewed sense of peace and purpose.

Looking ahead, I remained committed to nurturing my relationship with nature. I knew that life would continue to present challenges, but I also knew that nature would always be there as a source of solace and inspiration. The journey of connecting with nature was ongoing, and I approached it with reverence and joy, knowing that it was through nature that I could truly find healing and renewal.

The path ahead was illuminated by the lessons of nature and resilience, and I continued to move forward with a sense of harmony and wonder, eager to explore the boundless beauty and wisdom of the natural world.

THE STRENGTH IN VULNERABILITY

As my journey continued, I came to understand the profound strength that lies in vulnerability. For so long, I had equated vulnerability with weakness, believing that to be strong, I had to hide my fears, pain, and uncertainties. But life had a different lesson to teach me, one that would transform my understanding of strength and resilience.

The turning point came during a particularly difficult period in my life. I was facing multiple challenges simultaneously—work pressures, relationship struggles, and personal doubts. The weight of it all felt overwhelming, and I reached a breaking point. It was in this moment of desperation that I realized I could no longer maintain the façade of invincibility.

I decided to open up to a close friend, someone I trusted deeply. As I shared my struggles, I felt a mixture of fear and relief. I expected judgment or pity, but instead, I was met with compassion and understanding. My friend listened without interruption, offering support and encouragement. This experience was a revelation. It showed me that vulnerability could foster deeper connections and create a space for genuine empathy.

Inspired by this, I began to embrace vulnerability in other areas of my life. At work, I admitted when I didn't have all the answers and asked for help when needed. In my relationships, I shared my fears and insecurities, allowing others to see the real me. This openness was met with varying reactions, but overall, it strengthened my relationships and fostered a sense of mutual support.

One of the most significant impacts of embracing vulnerability was the way it changed my relationship with myself. I became more compassionate and forgiving towards my imperfections. I recognized that it was okay to have moments of doubt and weakness and that these did not diminish my worth or resilience. They were integral parts of my humanity.

As I continued to explore vulnerability, I found inspiration in the stories of others who had embraced this path. I read memoirs, watched documentaries, and attended talks by individuals who spoke candidly about their struggles and triumphs. Their stories resonated deeply with me, reinforcing the idea that vulnerability was not a sign of weakness, but a testament to courage and authenticity.

One particular story that left a lasting impact was that of a renowned artist who spoke about the role of vulnerability in creativity. She described how her most powerful and evocative works were born from moments of deep emotional exposure. This perspective resonated with my own experiences, as I had noticed that my most meaningful writing and creative projects emerged when I allowed myself to be vulnerable.

In embracing vulnerability, I also learned the importance of boundaries. Being open and honest did not mean exposing myself indiscriminately. It was essential to recognize when and with whom to share my vulnerabilities. I learned to trust my instincts and to protect my emotional well-being, ensuring that my openness was a source of strength rather than harm.

Reflecting on this chapter, I felt a profound sense of gratitude for the lessons vulnerability had taught me. It has shown me the strength of authenticity, the power of empathy, and the importance of self-compassion. The echoes of resilience, now intertwined with the wisdom of vulnerability, guided me with a renewed sense of courage and connection.

Looking ahead, I remained committed to embracing vulnerability as a vital part of my journey. I knew that life would continue to present opportunities to be open and authentic, and I welcomed them with an open heart. The journey of vulnerability was ongoing, and I approached it with curiosity and bravery, knowing that it was through vulnerability that I could truly connect with myself and others.

The path ahead was illuminated by the lessons of vulnerability and resilience, and I continued to move forward with a sense of authenticity and strength, eager to explore the depths of human connection and the power of being true to oneself.

Finding Purpose Through Service

One of the most profound realizations on my journey was the importance of finding purpose through service. While personal growth and self-discovery were crucial, I came to understand that true fulfillment often lay in contributing to something greater than myself.

This chapter of my life was about discovering the power of service and the ways it enriched my sense of purpose and connection.

The first step towards finding purpose through service was identifying causes and communities that resonated with my values and passions. I began volunteering at a local shelter, helping to provide meals and support to those in need. This experience opened my eyes to the struggles faced by many in my community and highlighted the impact of even small acts of kindness.

Through volunteering, I met individuals whose resilience and strength inspired me deeply. Despite their challenges, they faced each day with courage and hope. Their stories reminded me of the power of the human spirit and the importance of compassion and empathy.

Volunteering became a source of joy and fulfillment, allowing me to make a tangible difference in the lives of others.

In addition to local service, I sought out opportunities to contribute on a larger scale. I joined organizations focused on environmental conservation, social justice, and education. These causes aligned with my values and allowed me to use my skills and knowledge to advocate for change.

Whether it was participating in awareness campaigns, supporting policy initiatives, or educating others, I found a profound sense of purpose in these efforts.

One particularly impactful experience was working with a non-profit organization that provided mentorship and support to underprivileged youth. Through this program, I mentored a young girl named Maria, who faced numerous obstacles in her life. Our weekly meetings became a source of mutual inspiration. I helped her with her studies, encouraged her dreams, and provided a listening ear. In return, she taught me about resilience, determination, and the importance of believing in oneself.

As I continued to engage in service, I noticed a significant shift in my perspective. I became more aware of the interconnectedness of our lives and how our actions could ripple out to create positive change. This understanding deepened my commitment to service and reinforced the idea that we all have a role to play in building a better world.

Reflecting on this chapter, I felt a deep sense of gratitude for the opportunities to serve and the lessons learned through these experiences. Service has taught me the importance of empathy, compassion, and community. The echoes of resilience, now intertwined with the purpose found through service, guided me with a renewed sense of fulfillment and connection.

Looking ahead, I remained committed to the path of service. I knew that life would continue to present opportunities to give back and make a difference, and I welcomed them with an open heart. The journey of finding purpose through service was ongoing, and I approached it with dedication and passion, knowing that it was through service that I could truly live a life of meaning and impact.

The path ahead was illuminated by the lessons of service and resilience, and I continued to move forward with a sense of purpose and joy, eager to explore the many ways in which I could contribute to the well-being of others and the betterment of the world.

FROM FEAR YO GROWTH

Change is one of the few constants in life. This chapter delves into the experiences and insights I gained from embracing change rather than resisting it. For a long time, I viewed change with trepidation, associating it with loss and uncertainty. However, through my journey, I learned that change is often the precursor to growth, renewal, and new opportunities.

One of the most significant changes I faced was moving to a new city. The decision to relocate was driven by a combination of professional opportunities and personal circumstances. Leaving behind the familiarity of my hometown was daunting. The city had been my sanctuary, filled with memories, relationships, and routines that provided comfort and stability. Yet, I felt a persistent pull towards the unknown, a whisper that encouraged me to leap.

Upon arriving in the new city, I was confronted with the reality of starting over. Everything was different—the pace of life, the people, the environment. Initially, I felt disoriented and out of place.

However, instead of allowing fear to take root, I chose to embrace the change. I reminded myself that every ending is also a beginning and that this new chapter held the promise of new experiences and growth.

To acclimate, I made a conscious effort to explore my new

surroundings. I visited local cafes, parks, and cultural sites. I joined community groups and attended events to meet new people and build connections. These actions not only helped me integrate into my new environment but also opened my eyes to the beauty and vibrancy of the city.

One evening, as I walked through a bustling market, I marveled at the diversity and energy around me. I realized that change had brought me to this moment, a moment filled with possibility and excitement. This realization was liberating. It allowed me to let go of the past and fully embrace the present, with all its uncertainties and opportunities.

Professional changes also played a significant role in my journey. After years of working in a corporate environment, I decided to pursue a different career path that aligned more closely with my passions and values. This decision required a leap of faith, as it meant leaving behind the security of a stable job and venturing into the unknown.

The transition was challenging. There were moments of doubt and fear, particularly during times of financial instability and professional setbacks. However, each challenge was an opportunity to learn and grow. I discovered new strengths and skills I never knew I had. The process of reinventing myself was transformative, providing a sense of fulfillment and purpose that had been missing.

In embracing change, I also learned the importance of flexibility and adaptability. Life is unpredictable, and plans often go awry. Instead of clinging rigidly to expectations, I learned to adapt and find new paths forward. This mindset shift was empowering. It allowed me to navigate life's twists and turns with greater ease and resilience.

As I reflect on this chapter, I am grateful for the changes that have shaped my journey. They have taught me to be open to new experiences, to let go of the past, and to trust in the process of growth and transformation. The echoes of resilience, now intertwined with the wisdom gained from embracing change, guide me with a renewed sense of confidence and curiosity.

Looking ahead, I remain committed to embracing change as a natural and necessary part of life. I know that the future holds both challenges and opportunities, and I welcome them with an open heart and mind. The journey of embracing change is ongoing, and I approach it with anticipation and excitement, knowing that it is through change that we evolve and discover new facets of ourselves.

The path ahead is illuminated by the lessons of change and resilience, and I continue to move forward with a sense of adventure and possibility, eager to explore the many ways in which change can enrich my life and the lives of those around me.

THE POWER OF
FORGIVENESS

Forgiveness is a powerful and transformative force. This chapter delves into the journey of learning to forgive—both others and myself—and the profound impact it had on my life. Forgiveness was not an easy lesson to learn. It required confronting deep-seated pain, anger, and resentment. However, the process of forgiving brought healing, peace, and a renewed sense of freedom.

The first step in my journey of forgiveness was recognizing the burden of holding onto grudges. I realized that clinging to past hurts and resentments was not only detrimental to my relationships but also to my well-being. It kept me trapped in a cycle of pain and prevented me from moving forward.

One of the most significant experiences of forgiveness involved a close friend with whom I had a falling out. The disagreement had been painful, and the resulting estrangement left a void in my life. For years, I harbored resentment, replaying the hurtful words and actions in my mind. But over time, I realized that this resentment was consuming me, overshadowing the positive memories and the growth we had shared.

One day, I decided to reach out. I wrote a heartfelt letter expressing my feelings and my desire to mend the rift. To my surprise, my friend responded with equal vulnerability and a willingness to reconcile. We met, talked openly about our hurt and our regrets, and forgave each other. The process was cathartic. It allowed us to heal and rebuild our friendship on a foundation of understanding and empathy.

Forgiving myself was an equally challenging and crucial part of the journey. I had made mistakes and poor decisions that I deeply regretted. These self-recriminations weighed heavily on me, affecting my self-esteem and my ability to move forward. It took time and introspection to accept that making mistakes is a part of being human and that self-forgiveness is essential for growth and healing.

Through meditation and self-reflection, I learned to release the guilt and shame I had been carrying. I acknowledged my mistakes, made amends where possible, and resolved to learn from them. This process of self-forgiveness was liberating. It allowed me to embrace my imperfections and to approach life with a sense of compassion and understanding.

One particular moment of self-forgiveness stands out. It involved a career decision that had not turned out as planned. I had invested significant time and resources into a venture that ultimately failed. The failure felt like a personal defeat, and I was consumed by self-blame.

However, through reflection and support from loved ones, I came to see the experience as a valuable lesson rather than a defining failure. I forgave myself for the perceived shortcomings and focused on the growth and insights gained from the experience.

The journey of forgiveness also involved setting healthy boundaries.

Forgiving someone did not mean condoning their behavior or allowing them to hurt me again. It meant releasing the emotional hold their actions had on me and finding peace within myself. In some cases, forgiveness led to reconciliation, while in others, it meant moving on and letting go.

As I reflect on this chapter, I am grateful for the healing and freedom that forgiveness has brought into my life. It has taught me the importance of compassion, empathy, and the ability to let go of the past. The echoes of resilience, now intertwined with the power of forgiveness, guide me with a renewed sense of peace and understanding.

Looking ahead, I remain committed to practicing forgiveness in all areas of my life. I know that forgiveness is an ongoing process, one that requires intention and effort. The journey of forgiveness is continuous, and I approach it with dedication and grace, knowing that it is through forgiveness that we find true freedom and healing.

The path ahead is illuminated by the lessons of forgiveness and resilience, and I continue to move forward with a sense of peace and clarity, eager to explore the many ways in which forgiveness can transform my life and the lives of those around me.

REDISCOVERING JOY

Rediscovering joy was a vital part of my journey. For a long time, joy felt elusive, overshadowed by the trials and tribulations I had faced. This chapter delves into the moments and practices that helped me reconnect with a sense of joy and wonder, reminding me of the beauty and light that life offers even amidst challenges.

One of the first steps in rediscovering joy was reconnecting with my passions. In the hustle and bustle of daily life, I had lost touch with the activities that once brought me happiness and fulfillment. Music, for instance, has always been a source of immense joy for me.

Whether playing an instrument, singing, or simply listening to my favorite songs, music had a unique way of lifting my spirits and bringing me into the present moment.

I made a conscious effort to reintroduce music into my life. I dusted off my old guitar, started singing again, and created playlists that resonated with my current mood and experiences. Music became a daily ritual, a way to unwind and reconnect with my inner self. Each strum of the guitar, each melody, was a reminder of the joy that still existed within me.

Another practice that helped me rediscover joy was spending time in nature. Nature has a remarkable ability to soothe the soul and remind us of the simple pleasures in life. I began taking regular walks in the park, hiking in the mountains, and visiting the beach. These excursions provided a sense of peace and tranquility, a respite from the chaos of everyday life.

One particularly memorable experience was a solo camping trip. Surrounded by the beauty and serenity of the wilderness, I felt a profound sense of connection to the world around me. The sights, sounds, and smells of nature filled me with a sense of awe and wonder. I watched the sunset, listened to the rustling leaves, and marveled at the star-filled sky. In those moments, I felt a deep and abiding joy, a reminder that joy can be found in the simplest of things.

Gratitude also played a crucial role in rediscovering joy. I started a gratitude journal, where I would write down three things I was grateful for each day. This practice shifted my focus from what was lacking in my life to the abundance that already existed. It helped me appreciate the small moments of joy, from a kind gesture from a stranger to the warmth of the sun on my face.

One day, while reflecting on my gratitude entries, I realized how much joy I derived from connecting with others. Acts of kindness, shared laughter, and meaningful conversations brought immense joy into my life. I made it a point to nurture these connections, to reach out to friends and family, and to engage in activities that fostered a sense of community and togetherness.

Volunteering also became a source of joy. Helping others and contributing to causes I cared about filled me with a sense of purpose and fulfillment. Whether it was mentoring young people, participating in community clean-ups, or supporting local charities, each act of service brought joy into my life and reminded me of the power of giving.

Creativity was another avenue through which I rediscovered joy. Writing, painting, and crafting allowed me to express myself and explore my imagination. These creative outlets became a form of therapy, a way to process my emotions and experiences. I found joy in the act of creation, in bringing something new and beautiful into the world.

As I reflect on this chapter, I am grateful for the moments of joy that have enriched my journey. They have taught me the importance of staying present, appreciating the simple pleasures, and nurturing the activities and relationships that bring happiness into my life. The echoes of resilience, now intertwined with the rediscovery of joy, guide me with a renewed sense of lightness and wonder.

Looking ahead, I remain committed to cultivating joy in all areas of my life. I know that joy is not a constant state but a series of moments and experiences that we can seek out and embrace. The journey of rediscovering joy is ongoing, and I approach it with a sense of curiosity and openness, knowing that it is through joy that we find true fulfillment and happiness.

The path ahead is illuminated by the lessons of joy and resilience, and I continue to move forward with a sense of delight and anticipation, eager to explore the many ways in which joy can transform my life and the lives of those around me.

Living Authentically

Living authentically was a transformative part of my journey. For years, I had tried to conform to societal expectations and the opinions of others, often at the expense of my true self. This chapter explores the process of shedding those external pressures and embracing my authentic self, leading to a life of greater fulfillment and purpose.

The first step in living authentically was self-discovery. I needed to understand who I truly was, independent of the roles and identities imposed upon me. This involved deep introspection and self-reflection. I spent time examining my values, beliefs, and passions, asking myself what truly mattered to me.

One powerful tool in this process was journaling. Writing down my thoughts and feelings helped me clarify my inner world and identify the aspects of my life that felt out of alignment. I wrote about my dreams, my fears, and my aspirations. Through this practice, I began to uncover my authentic self—the person I wanted to be, not the person others expected me to be.

Another crucial aspect of living authentically was letting go of the need for approval. I realized that seeking validation from others was a never-ending pursuit that left me feeling unfulfilled and disconnected from my true self. I made a conscious decision to prioritize my values and desires over external opinions.

This shift in mindset was liberating. It allowed me to make decisions based on what felt right for me, rather than what I thought would please others. I started saying no to things that didn't align with my values and yes to opportunities that resonated with my authentic self. This boundary-setting was empowering and created space for growth and self-expression.

Living authentically also involved embracing my imperfections. For a long time, I had tried to present a polished and perfect version of myself, hiding my flaws and vulnerabilities. But this façade was exhausting and unsustainable. I learned that authenticity requires embracing all parts of oneself, including imperfections and struggles.

One transformative experience was sharing my story on my blog, "True Thoughts and Emotions." Writing openly about my journey, including the hardships and mistakes, was both terrifying and liberating. The response from readers was overwhelmingly positive. They appreciated my honesty and vulnerability, and many shared their own stories in return. This experience taught me that authenticity fosters connection and understanding.

As I embraced my authentic self, I noticed a profound shift in my relationships. Authenticity attracted like-minded individuals who valued and accepted me for who I truly was. I formed deeper, more meaningful connections based on mutual respect and understanding. The superficial relationships that didn't align with my true self naturally faded away, making room for genuine connections.

Living authentically also influenced my professional life. I pursued work that aligned with my values and passions, rather than simply following a conventional career path. This shift brought a sense of fulfillment and purpose to my work. I was no longer just clocking in hours; I was engaging in meaningful and impactful activities that resonated with my true self.

One significant decision was starting my own business, which allowed me to integrate my passions with my professional life. This venture was challenging but deeply rewarding. It required a leap of faith and a commitment to staying true to my vision, even when faced with obstacles and doubts. The support and encouragement from my authentic connections played a crucial role in my success.

As I reflect on this chapter, I am grateful for the journey of living authentically. It has taught me the importance of self-discovery, the power of vulnerability, and the freedom that comes from aligning with one's true self. The echoes of resilience, now intertwined with the commitment to authenticity, guide me with a renewed sense of purpose and integrity.

Looking ahead, I remain committed to living authentically in all areas of my life. I know that authenticity is not a destination but an ongoing practice of self-awareness and courage. The journey of living authentically is continuous, and I approach it with dedication and openness, knowing that it is through authenticity that we find true fulfillment and connection.

The path ahead is illuminated by the lessons of authenticity and resilience, and I continue to move forward with a sense of integrity and confidence, eager to explore the many ways in which authenticity can transform my life and the lives of those around me.

The Journey of Self-Love

Self-love was perhaps the most profound lesson I learned on my journey. This chapter delves into the importance of self-love and the practices that helped me cultivate a deep and abiding love for myself. For a long time, I struggled with self-worth and self-acceptance, often seeking validation and love from external sources. The journey of self-love was transformative, teaching me to nurture and cherish myself from within.

The first step in cultivating self-love was recognizing my worth. I realized that my value was not determined by external achievements or the opinions of others. My worth was inherent, simply by being human. This shift in perspective was empowering and allowed me to approach myself with greater compassion and kindness.

One practice that greatly aided in this process was positive affirmations. I began each day with affirmations that reinforced my self-worth and encouraged a loving relationship with myself. Phrases like "I am worthy of love and respect" and "I embrace my unique qualities" became daily mantras that gradually reshaped my self-perception.

Another crucial aspect of self-love was setting healthy boundaries. I learned to say no to things that drained my energy or compromised my well-being. This involved distancing myself from toxic relationships, declining commitments that didn't align with my values, and prioritizing self-care. Setting boundaries was an act of self-respect and a way to protect my mental and emotional health. It taught me that loving myself also meant honoring my needs and not overextending myself to please others.

Practicing self-care became another pillar of my self-love journey. This involved not just physical care but also mental and emotional nurturing. I made time for activities that brought me joy and peace, such as meditation, journaling, and spending time in nature. These practices helped me reconnect with myself and provided the space to reflect and recharge.

A key realization was that self-love isn't about perfection. It's about embracing myself as I am, flaws and all. I learned to accept my imperfections and recognize that they don't diminish my worth. This mindset shift allowed me to release the pressure of trying to be perfect and instead, focus on progress and growth.

Forgiveness played a crucial role in my journey toward self-love. I had to let go of past mistakes and the guilt I carried with them. Learning to forgive myself was liberating, as it allowed me to heal and move forward without being weighed down by self-criticism.

As I nurtured self-love, I noticed a positive ripple effect in other areas of my life. My relationships improved, as I was no longer seeking validation from others, but instead approaching them from a place of wholeness. I also became more confident in pursuing my goals, trusting in my abilities, and knowing I was deserving of success and happiness.

This chapter of self-love continues to unfold. Self-love is not a destination but a lifelong journey, requiring constant care, patience, and commitment. It's a practice that deepens over time, bringing more peace, fulfillment, and self-awareness with each step. The more I invest in loving myself, the more I can show up authentically in all areas of my life, cultivating deeper connections, achieving my goals with confidence, and living with a sense of inner peace.

Self-love has become the foundation of my personal growth, shaping how I navigate the world and the relationships I build. It has given me the courage to be vulnerable, to set boundaries, and to pursue a life that is true to my values and aspirations. Ultimately, this chapter is about the profound transformation that occurs when we truly begin to love ourselves unconditionally.

The Power of Transformation

Embracing change was a crucial part of my journey. Life is inherently dynamic, and learning to adapt and grow with change was essential for my resilience and personal development. This chapter explores the lessons I learned about embracing change and the practices that helped me navigate life's inevitable transitions.

The first step in embracing change was shifting my mindset. I realized that resisting change only created more stress and anxiety. Instead, I began to see change as an opportunity for growth and transformation. This shift in perspective allowed me to approach change with curiosity and openness, rather than fear and resistance.

One powerful practice that helped me embrace change was visualization. I started envisioning positive outcomes and new possibilities that change could bring. This practice helped me stay focused on the potential benefits and opportunities, rather than getting bogged down by uncertainty and fear. Visualization became a tool for manifesting my goals and dreams, guiding me through periods of transition with a sense of purpose and optimism.

Another important aspect of embracing change was developing flexibility and adaptability. I learned to let go of rigid plans and expectations, allowing myself to flow with the natural rhythms of life.

This involved cultivating a sense of presence and mindfulness, staying grounded in the moment while remaining open to new possibilities. Flexibility became a strength, enabling me to navigate life's twists and turns with grace and resilience.

Support from others played a vital role in embracing change. I leaned on my community of friends, family, and mentors, seeking their guidance and encouragement. Their support provided a sense of stability and reassurance, reminding me that I was not alone in facing change. Together, we shared our experiences and insights, helping each other grow and adapt.

One significant change I embraced was a major career shift. Leaving a stable job to pursue my passion was a daunting decision, filled with uncertainty. But I trusted my intuition and leaped, believing in my ability to create a fulfilling and meaningful career.

The transition was challenging, but it was also incredibly rewarding. It taught me the value of following my heart and trusting the process, even when the path was unclear.

As I navigated this career change, I focused on continuous learning and growth. I sought out new skills, embraced opportunities for professional development, and remained open to feedback and improvement. This mindset of lifelong learning not only enhanced my career but also enriched my personal growth, fostering a sense of curiosity and exploration.

Embracing change also involved letting go of what no longer served me. This meant releasing old habits, beliefs, and relationships that were holding me back. It was a process of decluttering my life, making space for new opportunities and experiences. Letting go was not always easy, but it was necessary for my growth and transformation.

One memorable experience was moving to a new city. Leaving behind familiar surroundings and starting fresh in a new environment was both exciting and challenging. It pushed me out of my comfort zone and forced me to adapt to new circumstances. But it also brought new adventures, friendships, and opportunities for growth. The move taught me that embracing change often leads to unexpected and rewarding experiences.

As I reflect on this chapter, I am grateful for the lessons of change. Embracing change has taught me to be resilient, adaptable, and open to new possibilities. The echoes of resilience, now intertwined with the courage to embrace change, guide me with a renewed sense of strength and flexibility.

Looking ahead, I remain committed to embracing change in all areas of my life. I know that change is a constant and that my ability to navigate it with grace and resilience will shape my journey. The journey of embracing change is ongoing, and I approach it with a sense of curiosity and adventure, knowing that it is through change that we grow and evolve.

The path ahead is illuminated by the lessons of change and resilience, and I continue to move forward with a sense of openness and optimism, eager to explore the many ways in which change can transform my life and the lives of those around me.

FINDING MY PATH

As I continued to embrace change, I found myself at a crossroads, ready to forge new paths that aligned more closely with my true self. This chapter delves into the steps I took to carve out a life that resonated with my deepest passions and values.

The first step in forging new paths was introspection. I dedicated time to self-reflection, journaling my thoughts, dreams, and aspirations. Through this process, I gained clarity about what truly mattered to me. I identified my core values and passions and used them as a compass to guide my decisions.

Setting clear and intentional goals became essential in this journey. I mapped out a vision for my future, breaking it down into achievable steps. This approach helped me stay focused and motivated, even when faced with challenges. Each milestone reached was a testament to my progress and a reminder of my resilience.

One significant change I made was pursuing a new career path that was more aligned with my passions. It required courage to leave the familiar and step into the unknown. But with each step, I felt a growing sense of fulfillment and purpose. The new path not only brought professional satisfaction but also a deeper sense of alignment with my true self.

Networking and building relationships within my new field were crucial. I sought out mentors, attended industry events, and joined professional groups. These connections provided valuable insights, support, and opportunities. They also reinforced the importance of community and collaboration in achieving my goals.

Embracing lifelong learning was another key aspect of forging new paths. I enrolled in courses, attended workshops, and continuously sought knowledge. This not only enhanced my skills but also kept me adaptable and open to new possibilities. Learning became a source of inspiration and empowerment, fueling my journey forward.

Overcoming fear and doubt was an ongoing challenge. At times, I questioned my choices and worried about the future. But I learned to acknowledge these fears without letting them control me. I practiced self-compassion and reminded myself of my resilience and ability to overcome obstacles. Each step forward, no matter how small, was a victory.

A pivotal moment in my journey was the realization that forging new paths often involved taking risks. I embraced the uncertainty, trusting that the journey itself would lead to growth and discovery.

This mindset shift allowed me to take bold steps, experiment with new ideas, and innovate. The risks I took often led to unexpected opportunities and profound personal growth.

As I continued on this path, I encountered setbacks and failures. But I learned to view them as learning experiences rather than obstacles. Each setback provided valuable lessons, helping me refine my approach and grow stronger. Resilience became my ally, guiding me through the ups and downs of forging new paths.

One particularly transformative experience was starting a personal project that combined my passions for writing and social impact. I launched a blog called "True Thoughts and Emotions," where I shared my journey, insights, and experiences. The blog not only provided a creative outlet but also connected me with a community of like-minded individuals. It was a powerful reminder that our stories have the potential to inspire and uplift others.

As I reflect on this chapter, I am filled with gratitude for the journey of forging new paths. It has been a testament to the power of resilience, courage, and self-discovery. The echoes of resilience, now intertwined with the pursuit of new paths, guide me with a renewed sense of purpose and determination.

Looking ahead, I remain committed to forging new paths that align with my true self. I know that the journey is ongoing and that each step forward brings new opportunities for growth and fulfillment.

The journey of forging new paths is a continuous adventure, and I approach it with an open heart and a deep sense of gratitude, knowing that it is through these paths that we find our true calling.

The path ahead is illuminated by the lessons of resilience, change, and self-discovery, and I continue to move forward with a sense of excitement and possibility, eager to explore the many ways in which forging new paths can transform my life and the lives of those around me.

The Power of Positivity

Positivity became a guiding principle in my journey, transforming how I approached challenges and opportunities. This chapter explores the impact of a positive mindset and the practices that helped me cultivate positivity in my life.

The first step in embracing positivity was changing my internal dialogue. I realized that my thoughts had a profound impact on my emotions and actions. By replacing negative self-talk with positive affirmations, I began to shift my perspective. I started each day with affirmations that reinforced my strengths, worth, and potential. This practice helped me build confidence and resilience, empowering me to face challenges with a positive attitude.

Gratitude became a cornerstone of my positivity journey. I kept a gratitude journal, writing down things I was thankful for each day. This simple practice helped me focus on the positives in my life, even during difficult times. It reminded me of the abundance of blessings around me and fostered a sense of contentment and joy.

Surrounding myself with positive influences was crucial. I sought out people who uplifted and inspired me, distancing myself from negativity and drama. Positive relationships provide support, encouragement, and a sense of belonging. Together, we celebrated successes, navigated challenges, and shared a mutual commitment to positivity.

Mindfulness and meditation played a significant role in cultivating positivity. These practices helped me stay present and centered, reducing stress and enhancing my emotional well-being.

Through mindfulness, I learned to observe my thoughts and emotions without judgment, allowing me to respond to situations with greater clarity and positivity.

Engaging in acts of kindness was another powerful way to cultivate positivity. Whether it was helping a neighbor, volunteering, or simply offering a kind word, these actions created a ripple effect of positivity. Acts of kindness not only made others feel good but also boosted my mood and sense of purpose.

One transformative experience was participating in a positive psychology workshop. The workshop provided tools and strategies to enhance well-being, such as practicing gratitude, setting meaningful goals, and fostering positive relationships. It reinforced the idea that positivity is a skill that can be cultivated through intentional practices and mindset shifts. The insights gained from the workshop became integral to my daily life, guiding me toward a more positive and fulfilling existence.

One of the key takeaways from my positivity journey was the power of perspective. I learned that how we choose to view a situation can significantly impact our experience of it. By adopting a growth mindset, I began to see challenges as opportunities for learning and growth. This shift in perspective allowed me to navigate difficulties with resilience and optimism.

Embracing positivity also meant letting go of perfectionism. I learned to be kinder to myself, accepting that mistakes and setbacks are a natural part of life. This self-compassion fostered a sense of inner peace and allowed me to approach each day with a positive outlook, free from the burden of unrealistic expectations.

A memorable moment in my journey was organizing a community positivity project. Inspired by the impact of positivity in my own life, I wanted to share it with others. The project involved creating a public art installation where people could leave positive messages and affirmations for the community.

The response was overwhelming. People of all ages and backgrounds contributed, creating a vibrant tapestry of hope and encouragement. The project not only spread positivity but also strengthened community bonds, showing the collective power of a positive mindset.

As I continued to integrate positivity into my life, I noticed profound changes. I felt more energized, motivated, and at peace. My relationships flourished, my work became more fulfilling, and my overall sense of well-being improved. Positivity became a guiding light, illuminating my path and helping me navigate life's ups and downs with grace and resilience.

Reflecting on this chapter, I am reminded of the profound impact that a positive mindset can have on our lives. Positivity is not about ignoring challenges or pretending everything is perfect. It is about choosing to focus on the good, finding silver linings, and believing in our ability to overcome adversity. It is about creating a life that is rich in joy, gratitude, and purpose.

As I look ahead, I am committed to continuing my journey of positivity. I know that it is an ongoing practice, one that requires intention and effort. However I am excited about the possibilities that a positive mindset can bring, and I am determined to embrace each day with an open heart and a spirit of optimism.

Facing Vulnerability

Embracing vulnerability was a pivotal step in my journey toward resilience and personal growth. This chapter delves into the power of vulnerability and how it transformed my relationships, self-awareness, and overall well-being.

Vulnerability, I learned, is the courage to be open, authentic, and exposed, even when it feels uncomfortable or risky. It is about showing up as our true selves, without the masks and defenses that we often use to protect ourselves from judgment or rejection. Embracing vulnerability was a radical shift for me, challenging my long-held beliefs about strength and invulnerability.

The first step in embracing vulnerability was recognizing the walls I had built around myself. These walls were constructed from fear, shame, and the desire to appear strong and capable at all times. But they also kept me isolated and disconnected from others. By acknowledging these walls, I began the process of dismantling them, brick by brick.

One of the most profound experiences of vulnerability was sharing my story with others. Whether it was through my blog, "True Thoughts and Emotions," or in personal conversations, opening up about my struggles, fears, and dreams was both liberating and terrifying. But it also deepened my connections with others, fostering empathy and understanding. People responded with kindness, support, and their own stories of vulnerability, creating a sense of shared humanity.

In my relationships, vulnerability became a bridge to deeper intimacy and trust. By expressing my true feelings and needs, I invited others to do the same. This openness created a space where authentic connections could flourish. It wasn't always easy; there were moments of fear and uncertainty. But the rewards were immeasurable, as my relationships became more genuine and fulfilling.

Embracing vulnerability also transformed my self-awareness. It required me to confront my fears and insecurities head-on, to sit with discomfort rather than avoid it.

Through this process, I gained a deeper understanding of myself—my strengths, weaknesses, and the patterns that shaped my behavior. This self-awareness became a foundation for growth, allowing me to make conscious choices and changes in my life.

One particularly powerful practice was seeking feedback from others. I asked friends, family, and colleagues for their honest perspectives on my actions and behaviors. This required vulnerability, as it meant opening myself up to criticism and different viewpoints.

But it also provided invaluable insights, helping me to grow and improve. It reinforced the idea that vulnerability is not a weakness, but a strength that allows us to learn and evolve.

Creativity and vulnerability are deeply intertwined. As I embraced vulnerability, I found myself more willing to take creative risks, to express myself through writing, art, and other forms of expression. This creative freedom was exhilarating, allowing me to explore new ideas and perspectives without the fear of judgment. It reminded me that vulnerability is at the heart of creativity, fueling innovation and authenticity.

A defining moment in my journey was participating in a vulnerability workshop. The workshop created a safe space for participants to share their stories, fears, and dreams. It was a powerful reminder of the universality of vulnerability—we all have our struggles and insecurities.

The experience was transformative, reinforcing the importance of vulnerability in building connections and fostering resilience.

As I reflect on this chapter, I am filled with gratitude for the power of vulnerability. It has been a gateway to deeper connections, self-awareness, and personal growth.

Embracing vulnerability has taught me that true strength lies in our willingness to be open and authentic, to embrace our imperfections, and to connect with others on a genuine level.

Looking ahead, I am committed to continuing my journey of vulnerability. I know that it will require courage and practice, but I am excited about the possibilities it holds. Vulnerability is a lifelong journey, one that invites us to show up fully and embrace the richness of our human experience. And as I move forward, I do so with an open heart, ready to embrace vulnerability and all the beauty it brings.

Forgiveness and Freedom

Forgiveness was another crucial element in my journey toward healing and resilience. This chapter explores how embracing forgiveness allowed me to let go of past hurts, cultivate inner peace, and build healthier relationships.

Forgiveness is often misunderstood as condoning or forgetting the wrongs done to us. However, I learned that true forgiveness is about releasing the hold that anger and resentment have on our hearts. It is a gift we give to ourselves, a way to free ourselves from the burden of past pain.

My journey with forgiveness began with acknowledging the deep wounds I carried. There were betrayals, disappointments, and injustices that had left scars on my soul. Holding onto these hurts had been my way of protecting myself, but over time, I realized that this bitterness was only causing me more harm. It was like drinking poison and expecting the other person to suffer.

The first step toward forgiveness was understanding that it was a process, not a one-time event. It required patience, self-compassion, and a willingness to confront painful emotions.

I started by writing letters to those who had hurt me, expressing my feelings honestly and without holding back. These letters were never meant to be sent; they were a way for me to release my pain and begin the healing process.

One of the most challenging aspects of forgiveness was forgiving myself. I had made mistakes, hurt others, and failed to live up to my expectations. Self-forgiveness required me to confront my humanity, to accept that I was not perfect and that I was deserving of compassion and understanding. This process was incredibly liberating, allowing me to let go of guilt and shame and embrace a more loving relationship with myself.

A significant breakthrough came when I forgave a close friend who had deeply hurt me. The betrayal had left me feeling angry and betrayed, and I had cut off all contact with them. But as time passed, I realized that holding onto this anger was preventing me from moving forward. I decided to reach out and have an honest conversation about what had happened. It was a difficult and emotional exchange, but it led to a profound sense of release and reconciliation. We were able to rebuild our friendship on a foundation of honesty and forgiveness.

Forgiveness also extended to my family. There were old wounds and unresolved conflicts that had created distance between us. By initiating open and honest conversations, we began the process of healing and rebuilding our relationships. It was not always easy, but the effort was worth it. We learned to understand and appreciate each other's perspectives, creating a stronger and more supportive family bond.

In my professional life, forgiveness played a crucial role in managing conflicts and building positive work relationships. Holding onto grudges or past misunderstandings only created tension and hindered collaboration. By practicing forgiveness, I was able to foster a more positive and productive work environment, where conflicts could be resolved with empathy and mutual respect.

Forgiveness also taught me the importance of setting boundaries. It did not mean allowing others to hurt me repeatedly or accepting toxic behavior. Instead, it meant releasing the anger and resentment while still protecting my well-being. Setting healthy boundaries allowed me to maintain my peace while engaging in relationships that were respectful and supportive.

As I embraced forgiveness, I noticed profound changes in my overall well-being. The weight of past hurts began to lift, and I felt lighter and more at peace. My relationships improved, as I was able to approach them with an open heart and a willingness to let go of old grievances. Forgiveness became a daily practice, a way to continuously cleanse my heart and mind of negativity.

Reflecting on this chapter, I am reminded of the transformative power of forgiveness. It is a journey that requires courage, compassion, and a willingness to let go. But it is also a journey that brings immense healing, freedom, and joy. Forgiveness is not about forgetting the past; it is about choosing to release its hold on us and embracing a future filled with love and possibility.

As I move forward, I am committed to practicing forgiveness in all areas of my life. I know that it is an ongoing process, one that will require continuous effort and self-reflection. But I am ready to embrace it fully, knowing that forgiveness is the key to inner peace and resilience. With each act of forgiveness, I am freeing myself to live a life of greater joy, connection, and fulfillment.

FINDING PURPOSE

Finding purpose was a central theme in my journey toward resilience and fulfillment. This chapter delves into how discovering my purpose gave my life direction, meaning, and a sense of belonging.

Purpose, I discovered, is not something that is given to us; it is something we uncover through our experiences, passions, and values. It is the driving force that gives our lives meaning and guides our actions toward something greater than ourselves. Finding my purpose required introspection, exploration, and a willingness to follow my heart.

The first step in finding my purpose was identifying my passions and interests. I reflected on the activities and causes that brought me joy and fulfillment. Writing was a consistent source of inspiration for me, a way to express my thoughts and emotions and connect with others. Through my blog, "True Thoughts and Emotions," I found a platform to share my experiences and insights, creating a community of readers who resonated with my journey.

Another passion was helping others. I found immense satisfaction in mentoring, volunteering, and supporting those in need.

This passion guided me toward opportunities where I could make a positive impact, both in my personal and professional life. Whether it was through community projects, charitable organizations, or one-on-one mentoring, helping others became a central aspect of my purpose.

Reflecting on my values was another crucial step. I considered what mattered most to me—integrity, compassion, growth, and connection. These values became the foundation of my purpose, guiding my decisions and actions. Living in alignment with my values brought a sense of authenticity and fulfillment to my life.

One transformative experience was attending a purpose workshop. The workshop was designed to help participants explore their passions, values, and strengths to uncover their unique purpose.

Through guided exercises, group discussions, and personal reflections, I gained clarity on what truly mattered to me and how I could contribute to the world in a meaningful way. The workshop reinforced the idea that "purpose" is not static; it evolves as we grow and learn.

As I embraced my purpose, I noticed a profound shift in my daily life. My work became more fulfilling as I pursued projects and opportunities that aligned with my passions and values. My relationships deepened as I connected with others who shared similar goals and aspirations. I felt a renewed sense of energy and motivation, driven by a clear sense of direction and meaning.

One significant realization was that purpose is not solely about grand achievements or major life changes. It is found in the small, everyday actions that align with our values and passions. Acts of kindness, moments of connection, and personal growth all contribute to a life of purpose.

This shift in perspective allowed me to find purpose in even the simplest aspects of my daily routine.

In my professional life, I sought out opportunities that aligned with my purpose. I transitioned into roles that allowed me to mentor others, lead projects that made a difference, and contribute to a positive work culture. This alignment brought a sense of fulfillment and joy that had been missing in my previous career pursuits.

Purpose also guided my relationships. I became more intentional about the connections I nurtured, focusing on relationships that were supportive, uplifting, and aligned with my values. This approach fostered deeper, more meaningful connections and a sense of community.

One of the most rewarding aspects of finding my purpose was the impact it had on others. By living authentically and pursuing my passions, I inspired those around me to do the same. Friends and family members began to explore their passions and values, creating a ripple effect of positive change. This shared journey of discovery and growth strengthened our bonds and enriched our lives.

The journey to finding purpose also involved embracing challenges and setbacks as opportunities for growth. I learned that purpose is not a destination but a continuous journey of exploration and evolution. Each experience, whether positive or negative, contributed to my understanding of myself and my purpose.

As I reflect on this chapter, I am filled with gratitude for the clarity and fulfillment that purpose has brought to my life. It has been a guiding light, helping me navigate the complexities of life with confidence and resilience. Purpose has given me a sense of belonging, a reason to wake up each day with enthusiasm, and a deep sense of satisfaction.

Moving forward, I am committed to living a life of purpose, continuously exploring and aligning my actions with my passions and values. I understand that this journey will evolve, and I am excited about the possibilities that lie ahead. With each step, I embrace the opportunity to make a positive impact, to grow, and to live a life that is true to who I am.

Living with Impermanence

One of the most profound lessons on my journey was learning to embrace impermanence. This chapter delves into the wisdom and resilience that come from accepting the transient nature of life and finding peace amid change.

Impermanence, the understanding that all things are temporary and constantly changing, was a concept that initially brought me discomfort. I had clung to the idea of permanence, seeking stability and predictability in a world that is inherently unpredictable.

However, as I faced various life changes—losses, transitions, and new beginnings—I began to see the beauty and wisdom in embracing impermanence.

The first step in embracing impermanence was acknowledging and accepting the reality of change. This acceptance did not come easily, as it required letting go of control and the illusion of certainty.

But as I began to observe the natural cycles of life, I realized that change is a fundamental part of existence. Just as the seasons change, so do our circumstances, relationships, and even our sense of self.

One pivotal experience was the loss of a dear friend. The grief was overwhelming, and I struggled to come to terms with the finality of death. However, through this profound loss, I learned the importance of cherishing the present moment and valuing the time we have with our loved ones.

The impermanence of life made each moment more precious, each connection more meaningful.

Embracing impermanence also brought a sense of liberation. It allowed me to let go of the need to control every aspect of my life and to trust in the natural flow of events. This shift in perspective reduced my anxiety and stress, as I learned to adapt to change with grace and resilience.

I found freedom in the understanding that nothing is permanent, and this impermanence allows for growth, transformation, and new possibilities. In my relationships, embracing impermanence meant appreciating the present moment and being fully present with those I cared about. It encouraged me to express my love and gratitude openly, to forgive more easily, and to let go of grudges.

Understanding that relationships, too, evolve and change, helped me to navigate conflicts and challenges with a more compassionate and open heart.

Professionally, embracing impermanence meant being open to new opportunities and being willing to take risks. It allowed me to view setbacks and failures not as permanent defeats but as stepping stones to growth and learning. This mindset fostered resilience and adaptability, enabling me to thrive in an ever-changing work environment.

One practice that helped me embrace impermanence was mindfulness. By cultivating a mindful awareness of the present moment, I learned to observe my thoughts and emotions without attachment. This practice helped me to stay grounded in the here and now, rather than worrying about the future or dwelling on the past. It brought a sense of peace and clarity, allowing me to navigate change with greater ease.

Another significant aspect of embracing impermanence was letting go of material attachments. I realized that my attachment to possessions and external achievements was a source of stress and dissatisfaction. By simplifying my life and focusing on experiences rather than things, I found a deeper sense of fulfillment and contentment.

As I reflect on this chapter, I am reminded of the profound wisdom that comes from accepting the transient nature of life.

Embracing impermanence has brought me a deeper sense of peace, resilience, and appreciation for the present moment. It has taught me to live fully, to love deeply, and to approach life with an open and adaptable mindset.

Moving forward, I am committed to continuing this practice of embracing impermanence. I understand that change is a constant companion on this journey, and I am ready to welcome it with an open heart.

With each new experience, I will find strength and wisdom in the ever-changing landscape of life, knowing that it is this impermanence that makes life so beautifully rich and meaningful.

The Liberation of Vulnerability

The next chapter in my journey was an exploration of vulnerability—a concept that, for many years, I had misunderstood and avoided. This chapter reveals how embracing vulnerability became a transformative force, deepening my connections and enhancing my resilience.

For a long time, I equated vulnerability with weakness. I believed that showing my true self—complete with insecurities, fears, and imperfections—would make me appear fragile and unworthy. As a result, I built walls around my heart, carefully curating the image I presented to the world. I showed strength and confidence, but beneath the surface, I often felt isolated and misunderstood.

The turning point came during a particularly challenging period in my life. I was dealing with a series of personal and professional setbacks, and the weight of keeping up appearances became unbearable.

In a moment of desperation, I confided in a close friend, sharing my struggles and admitting my need for support. To my surprise, this act of vulnerability was met not with judgment, but with compassion and understanding.

This experience opened my eyes to the power of vulnerability. It demonstrated that true connection and support are built on honesty and authenticity. By allowing myself to be seen—flaws and all—I created space for genuine relationships and meaningful interactions.

Embracing vulnerability became a practice, one that I incorporated into various aspects of my life. In my relationships, I began to share more openly about my fears, dreams, and struggles.

This openness fostered deeper connections and a greater sense of intimacy. It also encouraged others to be vulnerable with me, creating a reciprocal dynamic of trust and empathy.

In my professional life, embracing vulnerability meant acknowledging my limitations and asking for help when needed. This shift had a profound impact on my leadership style. Rather than trying to project an image of infallibility, I embraced a more collaborative approach, inviting input and feedback from my team. This openness not only strengthened our collective efforts but also created a more supportive and innovative work environment.

Vulnerability also played a crucial role in my creative pursuits. Whether writing, speaking, or engaging in artistic projects, I found that sharing my personal experiences and emotions resonated more deeply with others. It allowed me to connect with audiences on a human level, turning my struggles and triumphs into sources of inspiration and solidarity.

One of the most significant lessons I learned about vulnerability is that it requires courage. It takes immense bravery to show up as our true selves, risking rejection and judgment. However, the rewards far outweigh the risks. By embracing vulnerability, I experienced a profound sense of freedom and authenticity. I no longer felt the need to hide behind a façade, and this liberation allowed me to live a more genuine and fulfilling life.

A key practice that supported my journey into vulnerability was self-compassion. I learned to treat myself with the same kindness and understanding that I offered to others.

This meant acknowledging my imperfections without harsh self-criticism and recognizing that vulnerability is a natural and essential part of the human experience.

Another important aspect was setting boundaries. Embracing vulnerability did not mean indiscriminately sharing every detail of my life with everyone. It involved discerning when and with whom to be vulnerable, ensuring that my openness was met with respect and reciprocity. This discernment protected my emotional well-being while fostering meaningful connections.

Reflecting on this chapter, I am filled with gratitude for the transformative power of vulnerability. It has deepened my relationships, enhanced my resilience, and brought a profound sense of authenticity to my life.

Vulnerability has allowed me to experience deeper connections, greater empathy, and a more profound understanding of myself and others.

The Journey of Self-Acceptance

The next chapter of my journey focused on self-acceptance—a vital aspect of resilience and inner peace. This chapter delves into the process of embracing my true self, with all its complexities and finding contentment in who I am.

Self-acceptance began with a conscious decision to confront my inner critic. For years, I had carried the weight of self-judgment, holding myself to unrealistic standards and chastising myself for perceived failures. This inner dialogue was exhausting and undermined my sense of worth.

The turning point came during a period of deep reflection and introspection. I realized that the harshness with which I treated myself was counterproductive and damaging. It was time to cultivate a more compassionate relationship with myself. This shift required patience and a commitment to practice self-love.

One of the first steps in this journey was recognizing and challenging my negative self-talk. I began to observe the critical thoughts that arose and questioned their validity. Was it fair to hold myself to such high standards? Would I speak to a friend in the same way? This mindful awareness helped me to gradually replace self-criticism with self-compassion.

Another crucial aspect of self-acceptance was embracing my imperfections. I learned to view my flaws not as deficits but as integral parts of my humanity. This shift in perspective allowed me to accept my quirks, mistakes, and limitations as natural aspects of who I am. It was a liberating experience that reduced the pressure to be perfect and allowed me to be more authentic.

Self-acceptance also involved acknowledging my strengths and celebrating my achievements. For too long, I had focused solely on my shortcomings, overlooking the positive qualities and successes that defined me. By shifting my focus, I began to cultivate a sense of gratitude and pride in my accomplishments, however small they might seem.

One powerful practice that supported my journey of self-acceptance was journaling. Writing about my experiences, thoughts, and feelings provided a safe space for self-expression and reflection. It allowed me to process my emotions, gain insights into my patterns, and celebrate my progress.

Journaling became a form of self-care and a tool for nurturing self-love. In addition to journaling, surrounding myself with supportive and positive influences was essential. I sought out relationships that uplifted and encouraged me, distancing myself from those that perpetuated negativity and self-doubt.

The support and affirmation from friends and mentors played a significant role in reinforcing my journey of self-acceptance.

Another key element was practicing self-care. Prioritizing activities that nurtured my physical, emotional, and mental well-being helped me to cultivate a more positive relationship with myself.

Whether it was engaging in regular exercise, spending time in nature, or pursuing hobbies that brought me joy, these self-care practices reinforced my commitment to self-acceptance.

As I reflect on this chapter, I am filled with a sense of peace and contentment. The journey of self-acceptance has been transformative, allowing me to embrace my true self and live more authentically. It has enhanced my resilience, enabling me to navigate life's challenges with greater ease and confidence.

Moving forward, I am committed to continuing this practice of self-acceptance. I understand that it is an ongoing journey, requiring continuous self-awareness and compassion.

With each step, I embrace the fullness of who I am, knowing that self-acceptance is the foundation for a fulfilling and meaningful life.

The Strength of Community

The next chapter highlights the strength and support found in the community. This chapter explores how building and nurturing connections with others has been a vital aspect of my journey of resilience and growth.

Throughout my life, I have experienced the profound impact of community. Whether through family, friends, colleagues, or social groups, these connections have provided a source of support, inspiration, and belonging. The times of struggle and triumph, my community has been a constant anchor, reminding me that I am not alone.

One of the most significant aspects of building a strong community was recognizing the importance of reciprocity. Meaningful relationships are built on a foundation of mutual support and care. By giving as much as I received, I fostered connections that were deep and lasting. This reciprocity created a network of support that I could rely on in times of need.

In my professional life, I found strength in the communities I built with my colleagues. Collaborative projects, shared goals, and mutual respect created an environment where everyone thrived. These professional communities provided a sense of camaraderie and motivation, enhancing my resilience in the face of work-related challenges.

In my personal life, nurturing relationships with family and friends was a priority. Regular gatherings, heartfelt conversations, and shared experiences strengthened these bonds. Through these connections, I found a sense of belonging and unconditional support that was invaluable.

One particularly transformative experience was becoming involved in a local volunteer group. This community of like-minded individuals, dedicated to making a positive impact, provided a sense of purpose and connection. Working together towards common goals not only strengthened my resilience but also expanded my perspective and enriched my life.

Building and nurturing a community also involved being open to new connections. By stepping out of my comfort zone and engaging in social activities, I met new people who added depth and diversity to my community. These new connections brought fresh perspectives, opportunities for growth, and a broader sense of belonging.

Reflecting on this chapter, I am reminded of the immense power of community. The support, love, and strength found in these connections have been a cornerstone of my resilience and personal growth. My community has been a source of joy, comfort, and inspiration, reminding me that we are all interconnected.

Moving forward, I am committed to continuing to build and nurture these connections. I will prioritize reciprocity, openness, and intentionality in my relationships, knowing that a strong community is essential for a resilient and fulfilling life. With each interaction, I will embrace the opportunity to connect, support, and grow together, creating a tapestry of community that enriches and sustains us all.

Embracing Change

Change is an inevitable part of life, yet it often brings with it a sense of uncertainty and fear. This chapter explores my journey of learning to embrace change, finding strength in adaptability, and viewing change as an opportunity for growth and transformation.

For many years, I resisted change, clinging to the comfort and familiarity of the known. The unknown felt daunting, filled with potential risks and challenges. However, life, with its unpredictable nature, continually presented me with situations that demanded adaptability. It was through these experiences that I learned to see change not as a threat but as a natural and necessary part of my journey.

One of the most significant changes I faced was moving to a new city for a job opportunity. Leaving behind the familiarity of my hometown and the close-knit community I had built was incredibly difficult. The new city felt overwhelming, and I initially struggled with feelings of isolation and disorientation. However, as I settled into my new surroundings, I realized that this change was an opportunity for growth.

Embracing this change required a shift in mindset. Rather than focusing on what I had left behind, I began to appreciate the possibilities that lay ahead. I explored my new city, connected with new people, and gradually built a sense of belonging. This experience taught me that change, while challenging, can lead to new opportunities and a broader perspective.

Another significant change was transitioning to a new career path. After years of working in a corporate environment, I felt a growing sense of dissatisfaction and a desire for a more fulfilling and purpose-driven career. Making this transition was daunting, involving a leap of faith and a willingness to step into the unknown. However, by embracing this change, I discovered new passions and a renewed sense of purpose.

The process of embracing change also involved letting go of the need for control. I realized that while I could not always control external circumstances, I could control my response to them. This shift in perspective empowered me to navigate change with greater ease and resilience. By focusing on what I could influence and accepting what I could not, I found a sense of peace amidst the uncertainty.

Support from my community was invaluable during times of change. Friends, family, and mentors provided encouragement, guidance, and a sense of stability. Their belief in my ability to navigate change bolstered my confidence and resilience. This support network reminded me that I was not alone in facing the unknown.

Mindfulness practices also played a crucial role in embracing change. By staying present and grounded, I was better able to navigate the ebb and flow of life's transitions. Mindfulness helped me cultivate a sense of acceptance and curiosity, viewing change as an opportunity for learning and growth rather than a source of fear.

Reflecting on this chapter, I am filled with gratitude for the lessons learned through embracing change. Each transition, whether personal or professional, has contributed to my growth and resilience.

Change has taught me to be adaptable, to let go of the need for control, and to find strength in uncertainty.

Moving forward, I am committed to continuing to embrace change with an open heart and a resilient spirit. I understand that change is constant and that each new chapter brings with it opportunities for growth and transformation.

By staying adaptable and embracing the unknown, I will continue to evolve, finding strength and purpose in the ever-changing landscape of life.

The Practice of Gratitude

Gratitude has been a transformative practice in my journey of resilience and personal growth. This chapter explores how cultivating gratitude has shifted my perspective, enhanced my well-being, and deepened my appreciation for the present moment.

The practice of gratitude began as a conscious effort to focus on the positive aspects of my life. During challenging times, it was easy to become consumed by difficulties and overlook the blessings that surrounded me. By intentionally practicing gratitude, I began to shift my focus, finding moments of joy and appreciation even amid adversity.

One of the first steps in cultivating gratitude was keeping a gratitude journal. Each day, I took a few moments to reflect on and write down things I was grateful for. These could be simple pleasures, acts of kindness, or significant achievements. This daily practice helped to reframe my mindset, highlighting the abundance in my life rather than the lack.

Gratitude also involves expressing appreciation to others. I made it a habit to thank people in my life—friends, family, colleagues, and even strangers—for their kindness, support, and contributions.

Expressing gratitude strengthened my relationships and created a positive ripple effect, encouraging a culture of appreciation and recognition.

Another powerful aspect of gratitude was learning to appreciate the present moment. I discovered that gratitude was not just about acknowledging past blessings or future hopes but also about fully experiencing and appreciating the here and now. Mindfulness practices, such as meditation and mindful breathing, helped me stay present and cultivate a deeper sense of gratitude for the present moment.

Gratitude also played a significant role in building resilience. During times of difficulty, focusing on what I was grateful for provided a sense of perspective and hope. It reminded me that even in the darkest times, there were still things to be thankful for. This practice helped to build a foundation of positivity and strength, enabling me to navigate challenges with greater ease.

One particularly impactful experience was a gratitude retreat I attended. This retreat focused on deepening the practice of gratitude through meditation, reflection, and community sharing. Surrounded by like-minded individuals, I experienced a profound sense of connection and appreciation. This retreat reinforced the importance of gratitude as a daily practice and its transformative power in enhancing well-being.

Reflecting on this chapter, I am filled with a deep sense of gratitude for the practice of gratitude itself. It has shifted my perspective, enhanced my relationships, and deepened my appreciation for life. Gratitude has become a cornerstone of my resilience, providing a source of joy and strength in both good times and bad.

Moving forward, I am committed to continuing the practice of gratitude. I will cultivate a mindset of appreciation, acknowledging the blessings in my life and expressing gratitude to those around me. By staying present and focusing on the positive, I will continue to build resilience and find joy in the journey.

THE PATH OF PURPOSE

Finding and living with purpose has been a guiding force in my journey of resilience and fulfillment. This chapter explores how discovering my purpose has shaped my path, provided a sense of direction, and enriched my life with meaning.

The journey to finding my purpose began with self-reflection and introspection. I asked myself questions about what truly mattered to me, what brought me joy, and what I wanted to contribute to the world. This process was not always straightforward, and it involved exploring various interests and passions.

One pivotal moment in this journey was realizing that my purpose was not confined to a single role or career. Instead, it was about aligning my actions with my values and making a positive impact in whatever I did.

This shift in perspective opened up new possibilities and allowed me to find purpose in everyday actions and interactions.

Pursuing my purpose also involved taking risks and stepping out of my comfort zone. It required courage to follow my passions, even when the path was uncertain. Each step towards living with a purpose brought a sense of fulfillment and reinforced my commitment to staying true to my values.

Community and mentorship played a crucial role in this journey.

Connecting with individuals who shared similar values and goals provided support, inspiration, and guidance. Mentors, in particular, helped me to clarify my purpose and navigate the challenges along the way. Their wisdom and encouragement were invaluable in shaping my path.

Living with purpose also meant giving back and contributing to the causes I cared about. Volunteering, mentoring others, and engaging in social impact initiatives brought a sense of fulfillment and connectedness. These actions reinforced my purpose and provided a deeper sense of meaning in my life.

Reflecting on this chapter, I am grateful for the journey of discovering and living with purpose. It has provided a sense of direction, enriched my experiences, and strengthened my resilience.

Purpose has been a guiding light, illuminating my path and inspiring me to continue growing and contributing.

Moving forward, I am committed to continuing to live with purpose. I will stay true to my values, pursue my passions, and make a positive impact on the world. By aligning my actions with my purpose, I will continue to find fulfillment and resilience in the journey ahead.

The Legacy of Resilience

As I reflect on my journey, I recognize the legacy of resilience that I hope to leave behind. This chapter explores the impact of resilience on my life and how I aspire to inspire and empower others to cultivate their resilience.

Throughout my journey, resilience has been a constant companion, guiding me through challenges and helping me to find strength in adversity. It has shaped my character, deepened my relationships, and enriched my experiences. The lessons learned and the growth achieved through resilience are the foundation of the legacy I wish to leave.

One of the most significant aspects of this legacy is sharing my story. By openly sharing my experiences, struggles, and triumphs, I hope to inspire others to embrace their resilience. I have come to understand that vulnerability and authenticity are powerful tools for connection and empowerment. Through writing, speaking, and engaging with my community, I aim to create a ripple effect of resilience.

Another important aspect of this legacy is mentorship. I have been fortunate to have mentors who have guided and supported me on my journey. In turn, I am committed to mentoring others, providing guidance, encouragement, and a safe space for growth. Mentorship is a way to pass on the wisdom and resilience that I have gained, helping others to navigate their paths with confidence and courage.

Contributing to social impact initiatives is also a key part of this legacy. By engaging in causes that align with my values and making a positive difference in the world, I hope to inspire others to do the same. Whether through volunteering, advocacy, or community-building, these actions reflect the resilience and purpose that have been central to my journey.

Reflecting on this chapter, I am filled with a sense of purpose and responsibility. The resilience I have cultivated is not just for my benefit but for the benefit of others who may find strength and inspiration in my journey. By sharing my story, mentoring, and contributing to meaningful causes, I aim to create a lasting impact that extends beyond my own life.

The legacy of resilience is also about fostering a culture of empathy and support. In my interactions with others, I strive to be a source of encouragement and understanding. By listening deeply, offering a helping hand, and celebrating the successes of others, I hope to build a community where resilience is nurtured and valued.

Another important aspect of this legacy is lifelong learning. Resilience is not a destination but a continuous process of growth and adaptation. I am committed to remaining curious, seeking new experiences, and learning from both successes and setbacks. This mindset of continuous improvement not only strengthens my resilience but also sets an example for others to follow.

Gratitude is a cornerstone of this legacy. By practicing gratitude daily, I stay connected to the positive aspects of my life and maintain a perspective of abundance. This attitude of gratitude is something I hope to pass on to others, encouraging them to appreciate their journeys and the resilience they possess.

As I move forward, I am aware that the legacy of resilience is an ongoing process. It is built through daily actions, small and large, that reflect the values and lessons learned along the way. Each act of kindness, each moment of courage, and each instance of perseverance contributes to this legacy, creating a tapestry of resilience that can inspire and empower others.

A Future of Possibilities

As I look towards the future, I am filled with a sense of optimism and excitement. This chapter explores the possibilities that lie ahead, grounded in the resilience I have cultivated and the lessons I have learned. It is a celebration of the journey so far and an anticipation of the adventures yet to come.

The future is inherently uncertain, but it is also ripe with potential. Embracing this uncertainty with an open heart and a resilient spirit allows me to navigate whatever comes my way with confidence and grace. I have learned that resilience is not about eliminating challenges but about facing them with a mindset of growth and possibility.

One of the most exciting aspects of the future is the opportunity for continued personal growth. I am committed to pursuing new passions, exploring different paths, and pushing the boundaries of my comfort zone. Whether it's learning a new skill, embarking on a new career venture, or deepening my relationships, I am excited about how I can continue to evolve and expand.

The future also holds the promise of new connections and communities. I look forward to meeting new people, building relationships, and finding shared experiences that enrich my life.

These connections are a vital source of support and inspiration, and I am eager to see how they will shape my journey.

In addition to personal growth and new connections, I am passionate about contributing to positive change in the world. The resilience I have built equips me to take on new challenges and make a meaningful impact. Whether through advocacy, volunteering, or creative projects, I am committed to using my skills and experiences to make a difference.

Reflecting on the future, I am reminded of the importance of staying present and savoring each moment. While it is natural to look ahead and set goals, it is equally important to appreciate the here and now. The journey is as significant as the destination, and I am dedicated to living each day with intention, gratitude, and joy.

As I envision the future, I do so with a sense of hope and excitement. The challenges and triumphs of my past have prepared me for whatever lies ahead. With resilience as my foundation, I am ready to embrace the future and all its possibilities.

The Resilient Heart

The resilient heart is a powerful symbol of strength, courage, and love. This chapter explores the essence of resilience as it relates to the heart—how it endures, heals, and continues to love despite the trials it faces. It is a tribute to the enduring spirit that resides within each of us.

The heart is often seen as a metaphor for our deepest emotions and connections. It is where we experience love, joy, sorrow, and pain. Throughout my journey, my heart has been tested and stretched, yet it has also grown stronger and more resilient.

One of the most profound lessons I have learned is the power of forgiveness. Holding onto resentment and anger only weighs the heart down. By forgiving others and myself, I have lightened my emotional burden and opened my heart to healing and growth. Forgiveness is not about condoning hurtful actions but about freeing myself from their grip and moving forward with a sense of peace.

Love is another cornerstone of the resilient heart. Despite the heartbreaks and disappointments, my heart has continued to love and find joy in connections with others. Love, in its many forms—romantic, platonic, familial—has been a source of strength and resilience. It has reminded me that vulnerability is not a weakness but a testament to the courage it takes to open one's heart.

The resilient heart also embraces self-love. Throughout my journey, I have learned the importance of treating myself with kindness and compassion. Self-love involves recognizing my worth, honoring my needs, and being gentle with myself during times of struggle. This inner compassion has been a crucial part of building resilience, allowing me to bounce back from setbacks with greater ease.

Gratitude, too, is a vital aspect of the resilient heart. By focusing on what I am grateful for, I have cultivated a sense of abundance and appreciation. This practice has helped to anchor me during difficult times, reminding me of the good in my life and the strength I possess.

As I reflect on the resilient heart, I am filled with a sense of awe and gratitude for its capacity to endure and to love. The heart's resilience is a testament to the human spirit's ability to overcome adversity and find beauty and meaning in life's journey.

Moving forward, I am committed to nurturing my resilient heart. I will continue to practice forgiveness, cultivate love in all its forms, and treat myself with kindness and compassion. By doing so, I will honor the strength and resilience that resides within me, embracing each day with an open and courageous heart.

THE JOURNEY CONTINUES

As this book comes to a close, the journey of resilience and growth continues. This final chapter reflects on the themes and lessons explored throughout the book and looks ahead to the ongoing journey of life.

Writing this book has been a deeply personal and transformative experience. It has allowed me to reflect on my journey, acknowledge the challenges and triumphs, and celebrate the resilience that has carried me through. Sharing my story has been both an act of vulnerability and a testament to the strength that resides within each of us.

The journey of resilience is not a linear path but a continuous process of growth and adaptation. It is marked by moments of struggle and moments of triumph, each contributing to the tapestry of our lives. This book is a snapshot of my journey so far, but the story is far from over.

As I move forward, I am committed to continuing to cultivate resilience. I will embrace change, seek out new experiences, and remain open to the lessons that life has to offer. I will stay true to my values, nurture my connections, and pursue my passions with dedication and purpose.

The themes explored in this book—resilience, gratitude, purpose, love, and community—will remain central to my journey. They are the guiding principles that have shaped my path and will continue to do so in the future. By staying connected to these values, I will navigate whatever challenges come my way with strength and grace.

This journey is not one I walk alone. I am grateful for the support and encouragement of friends, family, mentors, and readers who have accompanied me along the way. Your presence and belief in me have been a source of strength and inspiration.

In closing, I want to leave you with a message of hope and encouragement. No matter where you are on your journey, know that resilience is within you. It is the quiet strength that endures, the courage that faces adversity, and the love that heals and connects.

Embrace your journey with an open heart and a resilient spirit, knowing that you have the power to overcome and thrive.

Thank you for sharing in my journey. May you find your path of resilience and discover the beauty and strength that resides within you. The journey continues, and with it, the endless possibilities for growth, connection, and fulfillment.

This concludes "Echoes of Resilience." If you would like to review any specific parts or need further additions, feel free to let me know.

The Excitement of New Beginning

As one chapter of my life closes, a new one begins, filled with endless possibilities and opportunities for growth. This chapter is dedicated to the idea of new beginnings and the excitement that comes with stepping into uncharted territory.

Life is a series of beginnings and endings, each one offering a chance to learn, grow, and evolve. Embracing new beginnings requires a mindset of openness and curiosity. It means letting go of the past and stepping into the unknown with confidence and hope.

One of the most powerful aspects of new beginnings is the opportunity to reinvent oneself. Each new phase of life provides a blank canvas, a chance to redefine who we are and what we want to achieve.

This process of reinvention is not about erasing the past but about integrating its lessons and moving forward with a renewed sense of purpose.

As I look ahead, I am filled with excitement for the possibilities that lie before me. There are new projects to undertake, new relationships to build, and new adventures to embark upon.

Each of these experiences will contribute to my growth and deepen my understanding of myself and the world around me.

New beginnings also bring with them the potential for new challenges. But with the resilience I have cultivated, I am prepared to face these challenges head-on. I know that each obstacle is an opportunity to learn and grow, and I am ready to embrace whatever comes my way.

One of the most exciting new beginnings in my life is the launch of my blog, "True Thoughts and Emotions." This platform will allow me to continue sharing my journey, connecting with others, and exploring the themes of resilience, growth, and connection.

Through this blog, I hope to inspire and support others on their paths, creating a community of like-minded individuals who are committed to living authentically and resiliently.

Another significant new beginning is my decision to pursue further education. Whether it's taking courses, attending workshops, or simply reading and learning on my own, I am committed to continuous growth and development.

This commitment to lifelong learning will keep me curious, engaged, and constantly evolving.

As I step into these new beginnings, I do so with a sense of gratitude for the journey that has brought me here. Each experience, whether joyful or challenging, has contributed to the person I am today. I am thankful for the lessons learned, the resilience gained, and the connections made along the way.

In embracing new beginnings, I am also reminded of the importance of staying present. While it's natural to look ahead and plan for the future, it's equally important to appreciate the here and now. Each moment is a gift, and by staying present, I can fully experience and savor the journey.

Reflecting on Resilience

As I continue to move forward, I recognize the importance of reflection in the journey of resilience. This chapter explores the power of looking back, not with regret, but with a sense of appreciation and understanding.

Reflection allows us to gain perspective on our experiences, to see how far we've come, and to acknowledge the growth that has taken place. It's a time to celebrate our achievements, learn from our mistakes, and make peace with the past.

In reflecting on my journey, I am struck by the resilience that has carried me through. There were moments when the path seemed insurmountable when the weight of challenges felt overwhelming. Yet, each of these moments was an opportunity to build strength, to learn, and to grow.

One of the most valuable aspects of reflection is the ability to see patterns and themes in our lives. By identifying these patterns, we can gain a deeper understanding of ourselves and our behaviors.

This self-awareness is a crucial component of resilience, as it allows us to recognize and address the underlying issues that may be holding us back.

Reflecting on the past also provides an opportunity to practice gratitude. Each experience, whether positive or negative, has contributed to our growth and resilience. By expressing gratitude for these experiences, we can cultivate a sense of appreciation for the journey and the lessons learned.

As I look back on my journey, I am grateful for the support and encouragement of those around me. Friends, family, mentors, and even strangers have played a significant role in my resilience. Their belief in me, their kind words, and their unwavering support have been a source of strength and inspiration.

Reflection also allows us to make amends and seek closure. By addressing unresolved issues and seeking forgiveness, we can free ourselves from the emotional burdens of the past. This process of healing is essential for building resilience and moving forward with a sense of peace and clarity.

As I reflect on my journey, I am reminded of the importance of self-compassion. It's easy to be hard on ourselves for past mistakes and short-comings, but true resilience involves treating ourselves with kindness and understanding.

By practicing self-compassion, we can nurture our resilience and create a foundation of self-love and acceptance.

A Vision for the Future

With a foundation of resilience and the lessons of the past, I looked to the future with a clear vision and a sense of purpose. This chapter outlines my aspirations and goals, and how I plan to continue building resilience in the years to come.

One of my primary goals is to continue growing my blog, "True Thoughts and Emotions." This platform will be a space for sharing insights, experiences, and resources on resilience, mental health, and personal growth. Through this blog,

I hope to create a community where individuals can connect, support each other, and find inspiration for their journeys.

In addition to my blog, I am passionate about writing and plan to publish more books that explore the themes of resilience and personal growth. Writing has been a powerful tool for reflection and healing, and I am excited to share my stories and insights with a wider audience.

Another important aspect of my vision for the future is giving back to the community. Whether through volunteering, mentoring, or advocacy, I am committed to making a positive impact and supporting others in their journeys. By sharing my time, skills, and experiences, I hope to contribute to a culture of resilience and empowerment.

Education and continuous learning will also be central to my future. I plan to pursue further education, attend workshops and conferences, and stay engaged with the latest research and developments in the fields of mental health and personal growth. This commitment to lifelong learning will keep me curious, informed, and equipped to navigate the challenges ahead.

As I envision the future, I am also focused on maintaining a healthy work-life balance. It's easy to become consumed by goals and ambitions, but true resilience involves taking care of our physical, emotional, and mental well-being. I will prioritize self-care, spend time with loved ones, and engage in activities that bring joy and fulfillment.

Finally, my vision for the future includes staying true to my values and living authentically. Resilience is about being true to ourselves, even in the face of challenges and adversity.

I will continue to honor my values, speak my truth, and live in alignment with my beliefs and passions.

THE JOURNEY OF RESILIENCE

As I close this book, I am filled with a sense of gratitude and hope. The journey of resilience is a continuous process, one that requires dedication, self-awareness, and a willingness to embrace change. It is a journey marked by challenges and triumphs, each contributing to the strength and growth that defines us.

This book is a testament to the power of resilience, the strength of the human spirit, and the importance of connection and community. It is a celebration of the journey so far and an invitation to continue exploring the endless possibilities that lie ahead.

To those who have joined me on this journey, thank you. Your support, encouragement, and shared experiences have been a source of inspiration and strength. Together, we can create a world where resilience is nurtured, where individuals are empowered to overcome adversity, and where we find beauty and meaning in our shared humanity.

The journey of resilience is never truly over. It is a path we walk every day, with each step bringing new opportunities for growth and connection. As we continue on this journey, let us do so with an open heart, a curious mind, and an unwavering spirit.

May you find strength in your resilience, joy in your journey, and hope in the possibilities that lie ahead. Thank you for sharing my story. The journey continues, and with it, the promise of endless possibilities.